A STORY BETWEEN THE LINES

Santhosh Sivaraj

Invincible Publishers

First Printing: 2019

ISBN: 978-93-88333-72-6

Invincible Publishers

Santhosh Sivaraj

Chennai, Tamil Nadu 600030

India

Edited & Typeset by: Dhivya Balaji, Precis Penning Literary Services (Chennai)

Cover Design by: Hamsapriya K, Infinit Solutions (Coimbatore)

To the Little Angels of Syria

Born out of love, but lost to hate

This book is not complete by the lines I write,

But by the colours you paint between them

Table of Contents

✦ ✦ ✦

Preface

I take this opportunity to thank my readers for saving my simple debut book 'The Blue Moon Day' from getting lost in the crowd of its counterparts, and also for giving me the recognition as a writer, which I cherish from the bottom of my heart. I believe my first book was a success because of the connect it had with the readers' life.

My eight-year-old nephew enjoyed the book as much as my sixty-year-old Professor friend, which was a proof of my belief in writing things in its simplest form.

I believe every word that was ever written resonates differently with every reader, based on their intellect and their imagination. And my words are no exception.

One interesting part of being an author is getting messages from the readers about various aspects of life, and I love reading every one of them. The common thing which I see from these messages, especially those from young people, is their wish to be someone who they are not at present.

Well, I don't have any problem with people having dreams and aspirations, but I feel it must not be at the cost of hating their present self which is special.

I would detail it with a little incident which happened with me a few decades ago. As a kid, I loved having pets (I still do – but I am no longer the deciding authority) and I had a dog named Tiger, a German shepherd.

This dog, in spite of being from that breed, never grew tall. In fact, it was growing long like Dachshund dogs. It also walked clumsily by spreading its hind legs making it the funniest dog in the neighbourhood.

I was unable to accept it, and was trying hard to change it, by making it do various exercises like jumping for the biscuits which were hung from a height, and so on. However, at the end of the day, the results were unfavourable, so I decided to call a dog trainer and was ready to spare my pocket money for his expertise.

The trainer spent some time with Tiger and informed me that it can't be treated, as the problem was inherent from its birth. He also played with Tiger for a while.

Before leaving the house, he told me that he had seen so many German Shepherds in his life, but none as special as Tiger. He was eager to buy if I was fine with selling it, which I never was. That incident is a lesson to me even today whenever I get stuck up in life's rat race.

A person's life is shaped by the choices he makes, and the culture he surrounds himself with. But if he messes it up by trying to be like someone else, then he essentially loses the real sense of being himself, which is unique.

I remember reading an incident that happened in Mozart's Life, one of the greatest musicians to have ever lived. A young man once approached Mozart, who was his inspiration, and asked him what he should do to become a musician like him.

Without hesitation, Mozart replied that the man cannot be like him, much to the young man's astonishment. He further said that he had never asked anyone to become the person he is now and this statement explains life's crux.

Life doesn't come with a definite set of rules to succeed, but when you start to believe that you are already who you aspire to be, things get easier and even happier.

To be happy, I believe it's always better to be at the bottom of the ladder you wanted to climb, than the top of the ones you don't.

Life is not a game of survivors where one lives on others' death. It is actually an abundant treasure, where there is space for everybody to live happily.

When trees can change their shape in search of sunlight, why should Man get stuck with his arrogant beliefs? He must remember that change alone is permanent and the rest shall pass.

With these thoughts, I thank you once again thank for helping me write, which I believe is my own way of making the world a little more beautiful.

In this book, I have taken the liberty of assuming a simple, common language being spoken by the characters throughout just to make sure the story crosses the lines and the hearts. The only other language the characters speak here is love.

✦ ✦ ✦

Editor's Note

I begin writing this note with mixed emotions.

I have read a wonderful book, and edited it, too.

I have been blessed to work with (on) a story that made me broaden my world view and my perspective of life's priorities.

A Story Between The Lines – is the most suitable title I have ever seen a book have in recent times. The story of the book is not just in the written words but the message they convey between those lines.

The first time I read the raw manuscript it took me a long while to understand its significance, though I was immediately bowled over by the plot itself.

And when I began editing, I noticed other subtleties. Each line had one of two purposes – to either further the plot or lay the foundation for the message that was conveyed. And the author, Santhosh, has managed this fine balance brilliantly.

The story cannot be conformed to any particular genres. There is love, there are emotions, there is a whole war that changes the lifestyle of people, and then there is the search for a truth bigger than life itself.

Amidst it all, there is a story between the lines.

What other losses does a man incur when he loses his memory? There is the obvious loss of his consciousness, the concept of missing major chunks of who he is as a person.

But there are also other losses that are not initially counted but have even more of an impact – like the sense of desolation and the frustration of having something just out of reach, tantalisingly close.

Life's trajectories are decided by our collective conscience and the decisions we make at every step of the way. Sometimes the most insignificant of decisions we make can bring about changes so big that we would not be able to trace them to that point of origin easily.

Adi's and Nila's lives go in that direction, all hampering on a few small series of decisions.

Empathy is a human quality so potent that makes life worth living even in war zones. While we see only the outwardly events that constitute a war, what goes on in the minds of the people caught in the cross-fire is something that can be brought out only via literature/cinema.

After everything is said and done, humans have the resilience that takes them ahead from the grimmest situations and keeps them going even when despair clouds them. This is the story of the people who, like us, had their lives, dreams, and ambitions. People who wanted to make it big, who wanted to make their mark in the world and achieve something they could be proud of.

What happens when life throws surprises at them? How do ordinary humans become extraordinary people in the face of life's oddballs? 'A Story Between The Lines' will tell you one possible answer to that question.

The book is a slow reflective read for a reason. It does not want to rush through life and get to a point. It would insist that the beauty of life is not its destination but the journey itself. Sometimes we all focus on our future and tomorrows, where every tomorrow becomes a today, and eventually keeping us suspended on the shadowy future, rather than on the steady present.

Adi and Nila are representations of who we are: people from simple backgrounds who find love in each other and plan a life together. They have dreams that bind them, and sorrow that holds them close.

But then there are other things that make them face their lives' toughest decisions. Maybe life is not about reaching the end, maybe it is about pausing to look at everything that leads us along the way.

And in that regard, this book gives you more things to take back, entire stories from between the lines that show us the different courses life can take. It is a mellow, emotional read, one you should savour and take in.

But it is also a reflective read, one that makes you wonder about everyday decisions you make that might have consequences beyond reach.

This book gives you the other side of the picture – the life behind the scenes, of action-packed war countries, of serene mountain villages with idyllic life structures, and of the incredible journey of people who persevere and make an impact so profound that they are remembered beyond life.

A Story Between The Lines is a book everyone should read because it will broaden your perspective on what constitutes as 'important' in the bigger scheme of things.

I wholeheartedly thank the author, Santhosh, for approaching me with this wonderful manuscript that has left a lasting, indelible mark on my psyche. An editing project is not just a book, but a learning experience for me.

Dhivya Balaji,

March 2019.

✦✦✦

When Dreams Are More Lucid Than Reality

Adi was on a military truck, driving on the lonely roads of a forsaken desert. He had no clue where the truck had come from and why he was driving it there. The frightening speed of the truck, that too on alien territory, made it impossible for him to think beyond the present danger. With every passing moment, the dangerous drive was getting monotonous. He felt like driving on a treadmill with a never changing terrain.

Unable to find a reason to continue driving, he decided to press the brakes and break the humdrum drive, but the wheels hardly responded to the pedals. Surprised by this, he pressed the brakes again, this time with all his might, but with the same result.

That was the moment he realised that he had no control over the vehicle. He was just a passenger in a vehicle, which was on autopilot. All this while, he had been busy in the driver's seat, assuming that he was manoeuvring a straight drive.

He started getting restless, as he was not sure what was happening and how he had come there in the first place.

Adi contemplated jumping out of the truck. But then the truck started to slow down all by itself. It came to a halt in the middle of barren land with nothing but orange sand all around. He was annoyed by the hopelessness of the place and decided to get back on the move.

He tried starting the vehicle, but the engines never cranked. Desperate to find an escape, he tried to start the vehicle once again by pushing it from the back but there was no sign of anything positive in spite of him repeating the process.

He got back into the truck to escape the direct sun, and leaned back on the seat, trying to make sense of the situation, when he saw a sudden movement in his side mirror. It was some kind of an animal that had crossed his view.

He got frantic at first but later decided to open the door to check it out. There wasn't any sign of the animal there, but interestingly he saw an oasis at a distance. He wondered how he had missed it during the dull drive.

Adi was approaching the oasis from the bottom of a slope. It didn't take much time to reach the bushes that marked the entrance of the oasis.

As he started to walk inside, he was surprised to see that the place was a lot bigger than he had imagined, that too in the middle of a desert. The more he travelled inside, the bigger it became.

Suddenly, he was face to face with a huge forest with its gigantic trees and a serene mountain at the back. The view was mesmerising, considering the agonising time he had had before. But yet, nothing made sense.

As Adi walked through the grasses, he felt that his shoes never touched the ground and he was quite literally floating amidst the greenery. With every movement inside the forest, Adi had this unique feeling that all the trees and the leaves were watching him anxiously.

He touched one of the tree barks on his way and sensed a wave of cool energy passing through him. He loved the feeling, and like a joyous kid, he moved ahead, spreading his hands and touching all the trees which he could on the way.

The more he saw the forest, the more he felt like he was a part of it. The feeling of oneness with the forest was too overwhelming. He couldn't move ahead anymore. He felt he was dissolving into this breath-taking nature; he sat on his knees and closed his eyes, with tears of joy rolling down his face.

It began to drizzle, making the place just right to be called heaven.

"Do you feel like you've lived this day a hundred times before?" asked a beautiful voice from the mountains.

Adi looked up and shouted excitedly. "Nila? Is that you?"

There was no reply, but he could hear a voice which silently echoed from the mountains, without falling into anybody's ears. He started running towards the voice, a deep whisper guiding him throughout.

Adi wondered if the whisper was actually within him. But he continued running, unable to doubt his heart. While running, he saw a magnificent rainbow extending itself across a waterfall and beginning to glitter as if it was signaling him the destination.

As he approached the spot, a cool breeze of fresh air invited him to the place and made his buoyant legs touch the ground finally. He saw a beautiful lady, with flowing hair, swinging gracefully using the roots of an enormous banyan tree, wildly across the falling waters. She looked at Adi and smiled as if there was no tomorrow.

"Nila, be careful. It looks dangerous out there," he said, caring more about her than her smile.

"Not anymore. You're here now!" She replied, swinging harder this time.

"Really?" he smiled.

"Do you remember what you told me the last time?"

“No!” He replied, still concerned about her swinging.

“You said to me – ‘just remember, I will be somewhere in the crowd with my eyes always on you!’”

He listened patiently, and asked, “But where were you? I was looking for you everywhere…”

“I was here Adi, living a ‘little life’ every day.”

“What?” he asked, unable to comprehend what she was saying.

“You were very far, Adi. I knew I had to wait long for you. So, I made my every day a little life, every morning a little birth, every evening a little wisdom, and every night a little death.”

“Am I dreaming?” he asked, with his hands on his hips.

“Well, I don’t think so. If you dream alone, then it’s a dream. But when we dream together, it is a reality,” she said with a wink.

“Did I take any medication or drugs?” Adi wondered if he was getting delusional by the sequence of events, especially Nila’s answers.

“Adi, now stop this and start observing yourself without any judgment. Believe in profound mystical experiences and don’t tag them with any rational explanations.”

“How can I? You sound like a fairy tale.”

“What stops you from believing a fairy tale? Nothing is a lie until it’s disproved. Who’s to say that dreams and nightmares aren’t as real as the here and now, what you think is the reality?”

“Let’s leave it at that, I can never win an argument with you. Now, come on, let’s go!”

“Well, it’s not that easy Adi. You have a long river to cross, and a tall tree to climb.”

“Are you serious?” he demanded and looked at the river. “Well, I don’t mind travelling the distance if nature is the only barrier. And interestingly you resonate with nature too!”

“Don’t make this mistake. Nature is a great deceiver. Remember that the deepest rivers flow in silence, and the tallest branches are always fragile.” She warned.

“So you want me to come or not?”

“I don’t think you have a choice. But remember, if you decide to set off on your own journey, you’ll find yourself alone for a long time. Are you ready for it?” She asked warningly again.

He was surprised by her constant warnings. “What makes you say that?”

“Well, I will answer your question if you answer mine.”

Adi kept calm for a while, unable to understand what was going on in Nila’s head. “Ok, ask me!”

“Tell me if you would rather lose all your old memories, or never be able to make new ones?”

Adi thought for a while and realised that the question was way deeper than it sounded. “What does my journey have to do with this question?”

“Well, this question summarises your journey. Every step you take towards me will make you lose your old memories, and at the end, you will forget your destination despite reaching it.”

“Why are you complicating things Nila? Why can’t you speak simply?” he asked, realizing that the discussion was getting way too complex.

"That's exactly what I am trying to do. Even if you have no idea where you're going to land, be brave enough to step up to the edge and listen to your heart, it will guide you."

"I will just listen to you, Nila, and not my heart."

"Isn't that my heart Adi?" she asked with a smile. "Even my love for myself came from yours!"

Adi gave Nila a mischievous look and asked, "What if I am late?"

"Well, I have learned to forgive all the apologies that I never get!"

"I hope you are not playing with me…"

"Lies look more truthful Adi. They come with more explanations, whereas the truth is too bland to accept, isn't it?"

"Oh, really? Let us see that. By the way, what if you are not there when I come?"

"Well, I remember your words – if you want the delight, then you must be ready for disappointments too!" She laughed softly.

"You sound like a riddle today, quite unlike you," he said, confused with the discussions and the journey he had to make again to get her back.

"Well my story is between the lines Adi, I am inside your mind and you reflect it."

"Just asking, can you take this journey towards me?" He asked eagerly.

"No Adi, my path is different now. I can't reach you from here."

He remained silent, looking at Nila, feeling that it was not just him, but even the rain and the rainbows had fallen in love with her. “Are you sure this is not a dream?” he asked once again, before taking a dive into the water.

“Even if it’s a dream, what’s wrong with that? Only dreams and nature are pure. Everything else is hell bent on conditioning you. You are your consciousness, Adi. In a state of unconsciousness, we are all just the same!” She said, turning away from him.

Hearing these words, Adi took a step forward, to jump into the water. He instinctively spread his arms before him, and incidentally pushed something cold and hard in front of him. It was a mirror, shattered into pieces.

That was when he realized he had been speaking to Nila’s reflection all this while. All the pieces of the mirror, irrespective of their size, carried his reflection.

He looked around, noticing that everything remained as before, except for Nila in the swing. He shouted her name repeatedly, only to hear an echo. He closed his eyes and decided to take the plunge into the water. He planned his course once inside the water and took a deep breath.

He jumped down headfirst and landed in the deep river, which was flowing faster than it looked like from the top.

Adi started swimming with the flow when he heard the same whisper again. Swimming with the waves, he looked up at the mountains and saw Nila standing there. He couldn’t speak or gesture as the raging waters kept him busy all the way. In spite of all this, he managed to get a glance of her with every desperate stroke of his.

With those little glances, he managed to see a scene of a lifetime. He saw that on the mountains, Nila was dancing around a tree with a little girl. They both were in white robes, looking like angels dancing serenely, unperturbed by the worldly woes.

With every move, Nila was looking at him with a smile. When he looked closely, he noticed that she was smiling, but her eyes were not.

✦✦✦

True Search Starts From The Self

Adi's eyes were closed, but his mind was trying hard to get back into the dream. He knew that once he woke up, this dream would slip away, and he would return to a clueless life filled with solitude and gloom. The more he willed himself to sleep, the more the restlessness crept up to him.

Agitated by this, he pushed aside his blanket and walked towards the balcony, trying to get some fresh air. The balcony too was lifeless, with dirt and dead leaves littering its floor, but it was still frequented by the birds coming to get a glimpse of their once favourite spot.

After roaming around in the balcony for a while, he walked back inside the house to make some coffee, which had been the only source of energy for most of his recent mornings. Every step he took inside the house reminded him of Nila. He recalled her sitting in a corner of the house once during a discussion, which now prompted him to rush to the spot and sit there, trying to feel her presence.

This was Adi's life inside the house, where he spent most of his time trying to make conversation with Nila's memories.

He made some coffee and sat on the swing which used to be Nila's favourite spot in the house. He was tired of thinking – in fact, tired of everything – as was apparent from his unshaven face, messed up hair and his filthy appearance.

He remained inside the house most of the time, waiting for that special knock on the doors that may come anytime. But today, he had some other plans. He decided to visit the police station, to get any updates which could be of some help to him.

Determined for answers, he wore his jacket, brushed his hair, and walked out of his house. Once on the road, he realized he was standing amidst a busy crowd, which made him feel even lonelier.

***

Adi reached the police station and was stopped by a smirking constable before he tried to enter the Inspector's cabin.

"Wait here! Sir will call you," said the constable trying to hide his smile.

Realising that the constable was ridiculing his situation, Adi asked, "What will happen to you when your wife disappears one fine day?"

The constable gave a disgusted look at Adi and entered the Inspector's cabin.

After a while, he came back and wordlessly gestured at Adi to go inside. Adi, however, was hardly bothered, as he was already perturbed with lots of questions in his mind.

"How are you doing now?" asked Inspector Dev, diverting his attention from his mobile towards Adi.

"I am good," Adi replied, taking his seat.

"Are you sure?" Dev asked again, looking more serious this time.

"What do you expect sir? How do I look? You tell me!" Adi voiced out his frustration.

"Hmm... So nothing new from your side I guess!" Dev shrugged.

"I came here to get updates from you, sir!" said Adi, trying not to sound furious.

"But Aditya, how can we proceed in this case until you help us?"

"I have already told you in detail all that I remember sir, now it's all in your hands!"

"This is definitely the most peculiar case I have seen in my career so far, where the husband loses both his memory and his wife. There has to be something which must spark the investigation, and it can come from your side alone." Dev said emphatically and paused. "So, did you have any recollection? Or do you suspect anything that can be of any use to us?"

"Nothing, sir!" Adi replied, frustrated. "I was at the hospital for a fortnight with no consciousness. On discharge, I rushed to my house, looking for my wife. I suspect that she might have gone in search of me, but she was new to this city… And I am worried something might have happened to her!"

"Stop this, Aditya! Don't start the same story again. Discuss facts – of what you know, and not your guesses and assumptions. I don't have time for your stories!" Dev said firmly.

"In fact, the hospital authorities informed us that you were picked up from the accident spot, which was very close to your house, and that you seemed to be already undergoing some treatment, which was apparent from the stitches in your head. Please try to remember if you got hurt or whether you got treated somewhere recently?"

"No, sir. For the hundredth time, no!" Adi replied, controlling his emotions.

"Okay, at least tell me the last clear memory you have!"

"I wish it was that easy for me to recall it. I could have carried forward with it. Anyway, I remember my marriage with Nila, and the days we spent after it. I remember my company wasn't doing well, but nothing more specific after that. The days are just jumbled together..."

"You and your wife were not at your house for the last 3 months. This was confirmed by the security of your apartment. In fact, we assume that you got into this accident while coming home… But again, what happened to your wife?"

Dev tried to start the discussion again. "We came to know that Nila doesn't own a cell phone. But even your call records confirm that you have hardly called anybody in the last three months' time, except for a couple of calls to your friend, which didn't help us much."

Dev continued, "You were also inactive on social media for quite a while. We tried locating Nila through the 'unidentified victims' list, accessing our recent accidental death cases, and also tried searching through the newspaper ads, but in vain. We informed the police department near her village to look out for her, but it was again a wasted effort. We even checked for your names in the divorce appeals registers in court. Now tell me, what else can we do?

Adi was agitated. "Divorce appeal? Sir, she is my life. How could you even think of that?"

"Listen, Aditya! You don't remember anything that has happened recently… And believe me, anything could have happened. If not for the doctors' certificate, we would not have believed you in the first place. It is usual in such cases to suspect the spouse first. That is standard protocol. In short, we're confirmation biased and most of the time, we're right. But yours is a completely different case, and all that we need to proceed further, in this case, is your memory. Any bit you can recollect will help us take it forward. Until then we're stuck with no way ahead."

"Sir, I know you are giving your best. But trust me, I'm living in hell every day. Only the hope of finding her is keeping me alive. Please help me, sir!" Adi's voice broke at the end.

Dev remained silent for a while. "Your friend had told us about you shutting down your company, and going on a break. All that we know is, you had taken Nila to her village, as confirmed by the people there. You stayed there for a while and left without telling anyone about your next destination. Anyway, I've already told you all this in detail."

"Sir, your description makes my life look clandestine… But believe me, I'm a normal guy, and Nila is a normal girl as well. We hardly had any secrets."

"Aditya, the memory you lost might have something crucial – even life-changing. But now you're back to square one. You don't really try to think anew, but you're trying to validate your existing views. Believe me, we were even sceptical about the very existence of Nila as an actual person, until it was confirmed by your friends and the people at the village."z

Adi remained silent for a while trying to get a hang of the situation. He stood up and asked, "So what should I do now, sir?"

"Don't keep thinking of what you already know and repeat the same endless frustrating questions to yourself. Ask different questions, and you will be able to find your answers in different places. Don't ignore any detail as irrelevant. Even the smallest detail may throw better light on your predicament. Come back if you still feel like you need our help," said Dev, looking at his watch.

Adi left the police station with more questions than he had had before entering it. However, they troubled him more this time, with zero help from the police. The constable, noticing Adi leaving the station, hurried into the Inspector's cabin.

"Sir, I think he must have murdered his wife, and now he is projecting this memory loss story to escape punishment"

"Well, the memory loss is true, and the doctors have confirmed it. Coming to his wife part, from all that I can see, he had loved his wife dearly, at least for the time which he could remember."

"Good for him, then," the constable sigh and got back to his work.

Once out of the Police Station, Adi felt hopelessness, hunger, and exhaustion further aggravating his emotions. He walked a few meters without knowing his next destination until he saw a roadside tea shop. Sipping his tea, he recollected the Inspector's words. The more he thought about it, the more he realized that it was left to him, and him alone, to find Nila… And he could only do that if he could remember more of what had happened. As the step forward, he decided to approach the neurosurgeon who had treated him after the accident.

***

Dr. Kurien was patiently listening to Aditya in spite of his exhaustion after completing two back to back surgeries.

"Ok Aditya, I have listened to you patiently. Now it's your turn to reciprocate," said Dr. Kurien. "Like I have informed you earlier, the condition you're suffering from is called retrograde amnesia, where you have forgotten events that happened before a trauma, although only for a specific period.

"Due to the injury, there have been some blood supply hindrances to the brain, causing some brain tissues to die. When the brain is damaged, as in your case, it can invent stories to help compensate for, and bring coherence to, a world that just doesn't make sense."

Dr. Kurien smiled. "Whether it's damaged by alcohol, diseases or even tumours, the brain can come up with absolutely fascinating explanations and parallel worlds to make everything appear normal once again."

"You mean to say I am living an illusion? What about the old memories which I have, doctor? Are they illusions as well?"

Dr. Kurien understood Adi's anger and frustration. He smiled. "Aditya, you came here for help, and I'm trying to help. But each case is unique even if it sounds similar. So ultimately, I will let you be your own judge"

"But doctor… Why possibilities? Why not a final conclusion?" asked Adi.

"That's because we're talking of the human brain here. It is a universe in itself. Even the possibilities which I'm giving now are based on the history of cases which were recorded and studied across the globe before."

Adi felt restless on hearing the doctor's detailed and composed explanation.

"Doctor, please don't mistake me. I'm too exhausted, and not in a position to comprehend a lot of things. Just tell me something that could help me, please."

Dr. Kurien smiled again, more to himself, realising that classrooms are way different from reality.

"Listen, Aditya. You had a brain injury that has erased a portion of your memories. The extent of the memory loss is still a question mark, as there is no real test to give a conclusive answer. There is some memory impairment, like Cryptomnesia, where you cannot remember when a particular event took place, or whether it was a dream or reality. Having said that, I must also tell you that you can't totally rely on other people's descriptions or explanations of your past. The fact is, other people won't remember events in your life as well as you do. Don't believe something just because you heard it from an authority. Do your research. Form your own judgment. Trust your instincts."

Adi could take in only the last few sentences of Dr. Kurien. But considering the fact that he was referring to his brain all this while, made him nervous. He was lost in his thoughts, wondering about the next course of action when Dr. Kurien got up from his seat, walked towards him, and patted his shoulder. "Relax. Don't push yourself too hard. Just trust your gut, it will guide you."

Adi rose reluctantly from the chair and thanked the doctor. While he was leaving the room, he saw a small note written on the doctor's desk.

'Some pay to lose their mind with alcohol, while others have it free for their whole life. Yet, people call them insane."

It was Adi's turn to smile.

***

Adi swung open the door of his house. He no longer bothered to lock it. He settled on the swing, recollecting the day. The discussions with the Police and the Doctor felt hollow, as there was nothing to take away from them that could have eased his present condition.

The feeling of helplessness was killing him. He kept going over the same thoughts repeatedly. No matter how desperately he tried for a solution, he was finally left with nothing but himself and his memories of Nila.

Complex thoughts started to overtake what was left of his sanity, and his emotions went on a rollercoaster of a rampage. He yelled and raged, smashing things all around the house until he was too exhausted to move. He fell on the bed with tears rolling onto the pillow. He continued to drain his sadness through his tears and slowly turned on his back.

He was looking at the picture he had taken with Nila in her tree house.

He continued looking at it when he noticed a diary beside Nila, which she used to write in every day. Adi's face brightened suddenly. He hoped that the diary might have some answers for him. It might hold the secret of why he had lost to the memory. His excitement dispelled the negativity abruptly as he stood up with a renewed vigour, deciding to get busy till he fell dead.

✦✦✦

Freedom Can Be Love

(The Beginning Of The Journey)

Adi was driving his 350CC bike on the rocky roads overlooking a green mountain. The hills were strikingly fresh from the morning rain. He had been on the roads for the past 3 months, trying to visit places with unique perspectives. He had left his successful corporate career to plunge into entrepreneurship. He had wanted to go on this self-introspective bike tour before plunging back to work again.

Riding the bike on long, winding roads was more like meditation to him, and he felt his brain worked better on the wheels than on his workbench. The trip had its own setbacks, like the bike getting repaired and overnight lodging issues. However, he valued the emotional experiences of freedom more than anything else.

Adi was entranced by the sight of the enormous mountain, with small houses built on it. He was amazed by the people living there and wondered about their way of Life.

He slowed down his bike and parked it on a green patch on the roadside. He poured himself some coffee from his flask and lit his fifth cigarette of the day.

Sitting on his stationary bike on the freezing hillside, overlooking the enormous mountain, with coffee in one hand and cigarette in the other, he felt bliss. He wanted the world to stay right there for the rest of his lifetime.

But unfortunately, all he could do was close his eyes, take a deep breath, and smile to savour the experience. He took out his SLR and tried to capture the moment, although he was not the kind who stored digital memories.

Adi noticed a herd of sheep marching in near-perfect, almost hallucinatory unison across the green patches, reaching for the water in the valley below. He was amazed at the discipline these sheep showed on the rocky pathway.

And he was reminded of the words of Nietzsche, a famous philosopher.

'The only way to escape the herd was to abandon the fantasy altogether and master your destiny by living for each moment and seeing the world for what it is.'

Nietzsche called those who were able to do this 'supermen'.

Adi wanted to be a superman too. He did not want to conform to the fantasy demanded by the herd, but instead embrace his individual non-conformity in all its rugged reality.

Adi took his cell phone from his bag and checked for the signal. To his surprise, the signal was good, considering the remoteness of the place. There were no important messages in his inbox, nor were there any calls.

He opened his Facebook page and was surprised to see the response he had received for his last status update. He had posted it while sitting in the catamaran in the middle of the sea.

There were hundreds of likes and plenty of comments, too much to go through. He decided to reply to the top few comments and leave the rest as such.

The first comment said, 'Awesome Bro, you are living an amazing life! You have decided to live life by your own terms… But for how long? Aren't you nervous about what's next?'

Adi liked the comment. It gave him the exact opportunity he had been waiting for. He replied.

'Four out of five bad things I've worried about never happened, but the four out of five bad things that did happen never occurred to my mind as things to worry about. If you are feeling nervous about going to a doctor, your nervousness won't actually stop after your appointment. Your brain will come up with the next new thing to worry about. I understood this and decided to live with it. I also chose to add a lot of cherished memories on the way!'

He read his reply again and loved the way he had framed it. He posted it and looked at the next comment.

'I want to be like you. But seriously I don't have time. Good that you are a bachelor! Or you'd be the one typing this comment!'

Adi smiled at the comment and 'liked' it as well. He remembered a statement his boss always said, which unfortunately had a different effect on him. He replied, 'If you don't plan your time, the world will plan it for you. It sometimes comes in the form of your boss, friend, family, your television, or even your bed!'

He wished his boss could read this reply and moved on to the next comment which asked, 'What is happiness, according to you?'

Adi paused and looked at the mountains. He replied, 'Happiness is when what you want and what you do are in sync.'

He glanced through the next few comments, which were predominantly on work, money, security etc. He stopped answering them, and instead posted an update based on his favourite saying of Marx.

He posted, 'Work is wage slavery. You have nothing to lose but your chains. Right is right, even if no one does it, wrong is wrong even if everyone does it.'

He switched off his mobile and decided to go for another cup of coffee. Sipping his coffee, he glanced at the herd again and noticed that all the sheep were eating with grace, in spite of their hunger. Maybe that was what the society was teaching us as well.

***

Adi packed his stuff into the bag and continued his blissful journey.

The mountains, the village, and the trees continued to amaze him throughout the journey until he heard a loud blast.

He stopped his bike, closed his eyes and said to himself, "Oh no! Not again!"

The rear tyre, which had recently been replaced after the previous one cracked, had burst open as well. The bad part of the tyre burst in bikes is that no spare tyres were readily available.

Even worse – Adi had just finished riding downhill and now it was all an uphill journey.

Adi got out of the bike, pulled out a cigarette, and looked at the mountains. They didn't seem very appealing now.

Realising that the cigarette couldn't help him much as well, he threw it off and started pushing the bike up the slope.

The uphill rocky mountain with its slippery roads was dampening Adi's mood. He could not even expect someone to help him with his bike in that remote area.

Sweating profusely, Adi was cursing the 200 KG of metal which he had to push all the way to the top, failing which it would reverse automatically.

Every inch of the bike's movement correlated with his mindless curses, which with time, extended beyond the bike's profile. He cursed his ruthless boss, his passionless colleagues, his brainless clients, and his parentless life.

Gasping vigorously, Adi moved on with his mindless blabber till he reached a point from where he had a good view of the valley. He saw a small roadside hut – his only solace, even if it just involved seeing a human life form.

***

After all the pushing, Adi reached the hut in one piece, still wondering if it was for real. He rested in front of the hut, and fell into a nap when a broken voice interrupted him. He opened his eyes to see an old man with two prominent teeth smiling at him. Adi woke up in a jiffy, quickly getting his bearings before saying anything.

He smiled at the old man, and in return, the man saluted him with a proud face, with some pride leaking between his teeth.

Adi's limited-edition military coat, short hair, and thick rubber shoes had made the old man assume he was a military man.

"I'm Adi. What's your name?" he asked.

"I'm Lal sir. I run the only teashop in these hills. Most of the locals come here for my tea."

"Then I guess you will have some idea about bike repair shops nearby."

Lal glanced at Adi's bike and was amazed at the sheer size of it. He had never seen such a big and complex bike, and he kept marvelling at it until Adi interrupted him.

"Did you hear me?" he asked, "Is there any bike repair shop nearby?"

"I don't think there is anyone here who can repair a bike like this. But I think you can find somebody in the city who might help you," replied Lal.

"Actually, I just need a tire repair and nothing else. Any idea where I can find a puncture shop nearby?"

"Sir today is a Saturday," Lal said with a sorry smile.

"So?" he asked, sensing something was amiss.

"All shops here will be closed till Sunday. You can get your bike repaired only on Monday."

Adi looked at him, wondering how to explain his situation in a crisp, simple way to him. "Are there any other choices?"

"Wait for the 3 AM bus tonight sir, it will take you to the city," replied Lal, also warning him that the bus can't be trusted, as the driver skipped the mountain route sometimes.

Adi got restless when he heard Lal's choices. Frustrated, he asked, "I want my bike's tire to be repaired now. What can I do?"

Lal shrugged and asked, "Sir, do you prefer tea or coffee?"

Adi got furious but realized that there was no point pushing his anxiety onto the old man. He decided to give it a break until he could come up with a better plan himself.

"Tea," he replied.

Lal smiled like a little boy and got into his hut. Meanwhile, Adi contemplated all possible ways to continue his tour but was left with little choice in the middle of the mountain.

"Sir, tea," Lal offered Adi's tea in a coconut shell.

Adi kept looking at the tea for long. It was the beverage's colour that intrigued him more than the way it was presented.

"Why is it orange in colour?" he asked.

"Sir, we make our own coffee powder," replied Lal.

"What? Is this Tea or Coffee?" Adi asked again, trying to confirm his order.

"Sir, it's tea only. But since you are from the high society, I added a little coffee powder so you will like it more," said Lal.

Adi had no reply for this. He felt harassed with a coconut shell of orange tea. He sipped it a little and found it hard to continue. He asked Lal to prepare coffee this time and emptied the orange liquid into the bushes.

Lal's coffee was better, and it helped Adi get rid of the orange coffee tea taste which was abusing his mouth.

While chatting, Adi came to know that Lal was fifty and had been living there all these years, doing the same thing.

"Don't you get bored, doing this all the time?" he asked, trying to understand Lal's life.

"Sir, apart from selling tea here, I also extract honey, cut wood, grow vegetables, maintain cattle and repair houses," Lal said proudly.

Adi was taken back on hearing Lal's answer and wondered if that was how people lived in the forest – doing many things at once.

"In my place, we do only one work. Even that, is decided by our society, and not us… By the way, you forgot the coffee powder job," he said, smiling at Lal.

Lal smiled back, unable to understand what Adi was trying to say.

"How much money do you make in a month?" Adi asked, sipping his coffee which had already become cold due to the weather.

"I don't know, sir. We don't need money for our day to day life, but we need it once in a while to buy clothes and things which we don't make ourselves."

Adi was getting a hang of Lal's lifestyle, fascinated to hear about the people living in the mountains. He said, "We people in the city love money, and there is never enough money for us!"

"Why sir?" asked Lal sincerely.

Adi smiled. "Because we always wait for that magical sum of money to appear for our growing needs, until it's too late to start living."

Unable to comprehend Adi's words again, Lal gave his trademark Dracula smile, indicating a 'whatever' by that gesture.

"I don't think I have any other option now but to visit your village, and your people, till I get some help," he said.

"You are most welcome, sir," replied Lal, excited.

Adi was surprised with his own decision. "I hope I'm not troubling you or the village people…"

"Not at all, sir. Our people love visitors."

"That's great. So, tell me, when can we visit the village?"

"Sir, I have to wait for my sheep to come back. This might take a while… I shall take you to the village after that!"

Adi nodded. "How do you go to your village?"

"It's through the woods only. We have made paths all across the forest for our commute."

"Do you expect any danger you while crossing the woods?" Adi asked.

"Not from this place, sir. The paths are made only on the safer route, and even our children roam around easily there.

One will encounter animals only at the mountain's base, where the woods are dense." Lal detailed.

Adi listened to Lal, wondering if he could make his way into the forest alone.

"Can I go to your village all by myself?" he asked.

"Sure, sir. It's a simple route. People keep visiting our village often. Just follow this road and it will lead you to the village." Lal pointed to a path.

Adi was excited to walk into the forest all alone. He parked his bike inside Lal's hut and packed his bag with all the camping gear.

"Are you sure it's safe?" he asked, confirming his decision once again.

"Definitely, sir. If you are afraid to walk alone, I will come with you." Lal offered.

"No Lal. It's alright. I want to do this, and again I never miss any first-time opportunity like this." Adi replied, and started walking towards the woods.

***

Adi was fascinated to walk through the dense jungle amidst gigantic trees with the smell of greenery all around. The last three months had been quite an experience for him, and he wished this jungle trip added some more flavour to it.

Based on Lal's description, he was expecting a broader pathway with very few hindrances. However, the path was too narrow for even a single person to walk through.

Adi kept walking for a while when he came to the first fork, where the pathway split into two. He didn't feel like walking back to Lal and asking for help, so he decided to take the route which appeared to be used more.

He continued to walk when he started to feel that he was slowly disappearing into the woods. He realized that he had covered quite a distance, but was yet to get a glimpse of the village.

To be more precise, he was yet to get a glimpse of anything at all, as he was always covered by the thick green shade of the trees which hardly gave space for even sunlight to touch the land.

Adi debated if he should turn back, which he felt would again take some time. He wondered if he was really close to the village.

With these mixed thoughts, he stepped forward, when he saw something crossing the path ahead. He didn't get a clear view of it, but he was sure that it was black, and like a big cat.

"Did I just see a panther?" Adi paused, shocked.

He stood frozen, sweating, with his heart pounding like hell. He remained rooted to that spot, and after composing himself, started to step back slowly. Once he reached a safer distance, he sprinted for his life, running with the adrenaline spiking his panic.

He continued to run until he realized that he was not only in a deep forest but also in deep shit.

Struck in the forest, Adi was losing his cool. His priority now was to not only escape the forest but get out safely before the dark. The thought of snakes and wild animals, especially the Black Panther in the deep jungle, was the last thing he wanted.

But unfortunately, all he could do was think and dread about them. He continued walking, hoping to see something encouraging. But except for his increasing helplessness, everything remained the same.

Tiredness was creeping in and Adi felt he had only a little time until which he could push himself. For a second, he thought of setting his camp there but the fear of wild animals made him take it back.

Irritated by the limited visibility in the forest, owing to the gigantic trees, he sat on a tree branch and sipped his water. He looked upon the tree in which he was, sitting and was startled that he couldn't even see its top branches. Then a thought struck him hard.

Why not climb that tree to see things from the top?

Climbing the tree was harder than Adi had imagined. He was hugging the tree tightly, as he feared falling down, more than actually climbing up. Slowly and steadily he was making his way to the top, but the branches got thinner with the height and were soaked from the day's rain, which made the climbing even more difficult.

Adi reached a point of support beyond which he found it to be impossible to climb. He looked around, standing firmly on that support. The forest looked just the same in all directions, as the view was curtailed by bigger trees and the complicated landscapes.

Adi felt disheartened and searched around just to get a hint of something good, but in vain.

Frustrated and angry, he hugged the tree once again and started his descent.

As he was getting down the tree, he felt he saw something bright amidst the trees. He stopped his decent and looked around, finding nothing. He trusted his impulse and decided to climb back a little and check again. He kept glancing around with every upward movement, and then it happened again.

He witnessed a bright light from the middle of a tree. Adi was overjoyed when he realized it was an actual tree house constructed in the middle of the forest. He continued to look at it, and almost shouted in joy when he noticed someone moving inside.

Adi descended in a jiffy, forgetting to hug the tree tight, causing minor cuts on his legs on the way down. He took his bag and rushed to the tree house, still trying not to make much noise.

***

As Adi neared the tree house, he felt a sense of poise in spite of the situation he had been in a few minutes back. Plants with attractive flowers were leading the path to the tree house.

Grass covered the pathway and bamboo wind chimes which were fitted around the tree were tinkling with subtle music, enriching the space with harmony.

In spite of the darkness all around, he felt this place to be an exception–not too bright, but glowing just right, like on a full moon night. Meticulously painted, captivating wooden carvings of animals and birds were placed all around the tree.

Adi felt like a spectator, witnessing a miracle amidst the woods. His fear was pushed aside by his curiosity and was getting restless to see the person who had created this heaven amidst the hazards.

He climbed the rope ladder hanging from the side, and slowly made his way to the tree house. The tree house was larger than he had anticipated and had paintings beautifying its entrance. The door was not locked, and the slow breeze was making it sway gently. Adi squatted on his knees to be even with the door's entrance and tried to peep in curiously. It was dark inside, except for the fading candlelight which was struggling to stay still.

Impatient to see if anyone was there, he slowly entered the tree house. But the darkness inside prevented him from exploring the place. He kept wondering about the movement he had noticed inside the tree house when a gust of wind gently opened a little window on the side. Adi could see the moon from that window, which also made its light spread through the room.

Adi's eyes adjusted to the dimness and he started noticing things inside the tree house. And that was when he saw the moonlight illuminating a beautiful face smiling in its sleep near the window. His heart skipped a beat on realising that someone had been inside already, but the innocent face sleeping cosily in a heavenly environment calmed him down immediately.

He felt peaceful. Watching her sleep was like visiting a still, peaceful pond on a starry night. He didn't want to disturb her, so he sat down comfortably looking at her, a smile on his face. He wanted the world to pause right there for the rest of his lifetime. Unfortunately, all could do was close his eyes, take a deep breath, and smile.

Adi was slowly pulled into a happy sleep by the chill winds and the warm floor when a loud clap of thunder made him sit upright, fully awake. The sleeping beauty was awake, and watching him, seated in a comfortable cushion. Once again, he panicked. But seeing the girl smiling at him, he felt calm again.

Adi was wondering how to begin a conversation and was even trying to figure out how to have a positive first impression on her. That was when she smiled again at him, like a long-lost friend.

"Are you a Trekker?" she asked.

He nodded more strongly than necessary to convince himself as well.

"Lost in the woods?" she asked again.

He shook his head. It felt way too easy to answer` wordlessly instead of explaining his nightmarish experiences.

"Don't worry, it happens sometimes. I am Nila. You are?"

"Adi," he replied automatically.

"Are you okay?"

He shook his head again, wondering how her simple questions make him feel so comfortable, putting him at ease.

"Can you speak more?" She asked with a smile.

"Yes," he answered. "I must say that the last few hours have been too strange for me to act normal."

"What happened?" she asked with genuine concern.

"That's a big story. To start with, I must say that I had one of the scariest moments of my life when I saw that animal," he said thinking of the panther.

"What animal?" she asked curiously.

"Panther," he answered with a serious face.

Nila thought for a second and replied, "That must have been a pig, not a panther."

That was the last thing Adi had expected to hear, but he persisted "It was a panther, I am sure."

She smiled. "Okay then. Let it be a panther. Are you happy now?"

Adi felt embarrassed in an instant and felt like a baby pig being coaxed. He could hardly come up with any justification for the existence of a panther in that jungle especially since he was not certain about it. He asked her, "How come you are so sure?"

She came close to Adi, looked into his eyes and said,

"Because this forest is my home."

He didn't try to interpret what she had just said, as he revelled in her proximity at that instant.

"So you came alone?" She asked softly.

"Well, yes. I am on an adventure trip, visiting places on my bike."

"You travel by bike everywhere?"

"Yeah, I go to places which are accessible on a bike"

"Then how come you're here?" she asked again.

Adi realised that he couldn't skip his story now, and briefed everything, starting with the reason for his self-realization trip.

Nila loved listening to Adi's story and was impressed by his outlook on life. She wanted to know more and kept asking him in detail about his trip. Adi felt comfortable speaking to her, too, and shared his experiences to his heart's content.

"Why are you doing it all alone? Why don't you have company?" she asked.

"Well I haven't thought much about that, but I do keep updating my whereabouts to my friends. And none of them seem to be interested in a journey like this."

"Why not? I mean, I feel jealous, looking at you," she said.

Adi smiled at her and felt as if he had known her for ages.

"Would you like to see my photos?" he asked.

Nila nodded like a little girl and moved closer to him. She started looking at the pictures through the camera, which was a first for her. She was amazed at the technology, but curbed her enthusiasm, trying not to look childish.

While looking at one of the pictures, she exclaimed, "Are you flying?"

Adi smiled. "Not really. It's called sky diving. I just jumped from a plane."

"Really, weren't you afraid? I can't believe this," she said excitedly.

"Well a small fear was there at the beginning, but otherwise it was fine," he replied a bit hesitantly.

Nila acknowledged and kept looking at the pictures, operating the camera herself this time when Adi interrupted.

"Nila, I am sorry I just told you a lie."

She looked at him questioningly.

"I was actually terrified of sky diving, and I could hardly jump out from the plane. That was when somebody pushed me from the back. During the freefall, I went blank and also ended up vomiting all over myself and my guide!" he said without a break and felt redeemed of his lies.

Nila smiled first, which eventually turned into uncontrollable laughter. She couldn't help but imagine Adi vomiting in the sky. She liked the way he had told her the truth, though it was not necessary.

"Do you have any more stories like this?" she asked.

"In fact, I do!" he said excitedly. "There was this holy place near the Himalayas where people frequent an ashram. I went there to check it out. I had no clue about that place and mistakenly ended up in a room where the main saint lived."

"Then?" asked Nila, unable to control her curiosity.

"Well, I entered the room at a wrong time, when I saw the saint in an elated state with smoke all over the room!"

"What? I don't get you!" she said, unable to understand what he was referring to.

"Well, can't dwell more on that, but all I can say was that I gave him a towel and he gave me a joint. After a while, when the devotees opened the room, they saw two smiling saints, similarly dressed, dancing to their own tunes!"

Nila laughed uncontrollably again and patted Adi on his shoulders.

"Anything else?" she asked again.

He looked at her and said, "Nila, this is my self-realization tour and not any random trip where I clown around. But yes, there was a time when I actually looked like a clown, with a red bulging nose, when a bee stung it during my nap under a tree. The worst part was that my food and money were also stolen, and I became a clown beggar that afternoon."

Nila continued to laugh, absolutely loving the talk.

Adi found her incredibly attractive. She apparently understood her core, which made her fully present in every moment, not distracted by worldly worries. He realized for the first time that beauty in emotions and expressions were far more real than those static ones that were skin deep.

Nila sat calmly thinking for a while. "Why do you do all this? You know sometimes it can be dangerous too."

"I don't do these things to surpass fear or feel independent but to feel something which I have never felt before. It's difficult for me to put it in words, Nila."

"I understand what you meant by inexplicable emotions. I feel the same when I look at the stars at night, lying on the pond side. It calms me, helping me forget whatever problem I have, and makes me feel like I'm living above everything..."

Nila continued speaking about that while Adi was busy

adoring her, where even her chicken pox scar on the cheeks looked like dimples to him.

"Will you come to the pond with me now?" she asked him, wanting him to actually experience what she had just said.

"Why not? But is it safe at this hour of the night?"

Nila smiled at him, held his hands, and took him with her. They reached the pond near the tree house.

"I am planning to create a little universe, around the pond and my tree house, by diverting a little water from this stream. Maybe the next time you come, it will be exquisite, with more lives living thriving here."

Nila immersed her feet into the pond.

Adi felt the place to be calming and rejuvenating. It also made him wonder about its beauty, especially with Nila nearby. They both lied down on the pond side, staring at the stars. They continued to talk for a while when he realized that his words had become a lullaby as she slept peacefully beside him.

Adi, however, couldn't sleep.

He was still smiling at the stars and was eagerly waiting for one to shoot across the sky so he could make a wish. He looked at Nila. The fact that she did not care made her more attractive to him. It also bugged him that he was falling in love with a girl who was just sleeping.

But deep down, he knew that his solo trip had come to an end. He had found a lifelong companion, and until she joined him on his journey, his destination will be hers.

***

"Wake up Adi, its morning already," said Nila, shaking him up gently from his dream.

Adi was too reluctant to open his eyes, but when he realized where he was, he woke up in a hurry and made sure Nila was nearby.

"Are you alright?" he asked.

She gave an engaging smile. "Yes, how about you?"

Realising that it was the first time in his life he had woken up with a girl beside him, he replied "Never better!"

"Great! So, would you like to visit my village, or do you want to get back to your trip?"

"You said this is your home! I mean… The forest…" he exclaimed, a little perplexed.

She smiled, "I am not a jungle dweller. I live in the village. But yes, I like the forest, and that's why I've made myself a little home here."

"Would you mind sharing it with me?" Adi asked, impulsively.

She just nodded, smiling.

Together, they starting walking towards the village. During the course of their walk, Adi realized that Nila was taking the same route which had led him to her. When they came to a junction, he realised he had taken a wrong fork there.

A fallen tree had hidden the obvious road, which led to the village in no time. As they were removing the tree from the roads, he heard a voice from behind. It was Lal, who had been looking for Adi in the woods. Lal's eyes were teary as he approached Adi, and hugged him tightly.

Adi understood what had just happened, and was amazed at the concern Lal had for him. His eyes got moist as well. It was a moment to cherish when someone who he hardly knew cried for him.

"I am sorry. I should have gone with you," Lal said.

"Please don't worry! Believe me, everything was perfect!" Adi replied trying not to talk more about the previous night

Lal informed that two of his sheep had gone missing, because of which he had not gone to the village that night. He had stayed back at his shop, or else, he declared, the villagers would have searched for Adi in the forest since the night itself!

Lal saw Nila standing behind Adi, and they discussed the events that happened the day before as they continued walking towards the village.

During the walk, Nila called Adi and pointed out a fat pig which was running into the bushes. "Look, Adi! There is your panther!"

Adi just blushed, and Lal joined in the laughter when Nila told him the panther story.

As they approached the village, Adi saw a group of people standing near the entrance, smiling at their arrival. They had obviously been anxious about Adi's return and welcomed him with a garland, which made him feel comfortable amidst them.

Lal said, "I told them about you, and they were preparing to enter the forest to find you… By sending search parties inside."

Adi got emotional at the love and concern of the village people. He could hardly remember any other time in his life so far where he had mattered so much to so many people. He was offered a special breakfast, during which he found Nila missing. It made him restless and finish his breakfast hurriedly despite Lal's repeated requests to have more. He walked out to the open space and looked at the little houses built on the hilly rocks. He was looking for Nila, but nobody was there.

He approached Lal and asked, "Where does Nila live?"

Lal smiled, harassing the food between his complex teeth, and pointed to a little hut which was located at the peak of the mountain with green pastures all around.

Hesitating slightly, Adi proceeded towards Nila's house and knocked.

Nila opened the door and smiled gracefully on seeing Adi. She was dressed beautifully in orange, and her contagious smile never allowed Adi to take his eyes off her.

He had no idea of what to talk, in spite of their marathon discussions the night before.

Nila offered him tea and remained silent, unable to start any conversation.

Adi broke the silence. "Your village is so beautiful. And so are the people. I love the way they welcomed me, although I am terrified of their pigs!"

Nila smiled. "No, it was a panther!"

She was pulling his leg. While they were talking, Nila's grandfather, Ranga entered the house.

Nila introduced Adi to her grandfather and they began chatting.

During the chat, Adi came to know that Nila was raised all alone by her grandfather, who was a courteous man full of wisdom and had been instrumental in the village's welfare and development.

After a while, Ranga asked Adi, "So what is your plan?"

Adi asked back "Plan for what?"

"Life," said Ranga, smiling serenely, looking forward to the answer.

Adi started to speak about his entrepreneurship plans, his early retirement, and also about his social service intentions to the needy after that.

Ranga nodded and asked, "Anything left unplanned?"

"Not really" Adi replied, although the question surprised him.

"Don't plan so much so young. Give chance for surprises in your life, like what happened today." Ranga said calmly.

Adi nodded his head, amazed at the advice he had received from an old man living on top of a mountain.

"So, when are you leaving?" asked Ranga.

Adi found it tough to answer, as he was keen on spending some more time with Nila. "Not yet decided sir. Maybe tomorrow," he answered, finding the word 'tomorrow' to be too disturbing suddenly.

"That's great. I shall arrange for a special dinner tonight," Ranga said and excused himself.

"Why are you going so soon?" asked Nila, who had been listening from the kitchen.

Adi couldn't answer her, but he knew he had just curtailed himself, with too little time to convey his feeling for her.

Throughout the course of the day, Adi explored the village with Nila accompanying him. He realised that the people there loved Nila, and she was the life of the village. She knew everyone personally and cared for them with her heart. She was the interior and exterior decorator of the village, as she loved making clay structures, paintings and all sort of things that can beautify the space around her.

She took Adi to her tree house again and showed him things which he had missed in the darkness of the previous night.

The more Adi thought he had understood Nila, the more mysterious she seemed. She had created her own beautiful world where she spoke to trees and animals. She loved beautifying the world around her and prayed to the almighty for everything except herself.

She was the only vegetarian in the forest, and interestingly, she had no problems with others consuming meat.

Every second with Nila was like living a surreal dream for him, in spite of knowing that she was a village girl who had nothing but happiness, whereas he had everything but Nila.

Adi decided to convey his feelings for her, although he was afraid that she might not reciprocate. He also felt that he should give her a chance to make the decision and not come to a conclusion all by himself only to regret it later.

Nila was showing him her diary she usually kept hidden in the tree house, in which she had written her dreams for the next day.

Adi hardly bothered about the diary and the hiding spot. He was keenly waiting for the right time to propose to her. He kept missing all the opportunities, and finally, it was dusk. Nila was taking Adi to the dinner feast which was arranged at the centre of the village, beside a big campfire. Adi could not control the feeling of melancholy in leaving the village the next day.

The mere thought of bidding goodbye to Nila was hurting him.

The whole village had gathered for the feast, and everyone was seated evenly around the campfire with the centre place reserved for Adi, their special guest for the day. Music was played with homemade instruments. Adi was looking at the gathering, noticing that everyone was smiling.

The music, the campfire, the mountains, and the people, everything was just perfect.

He thought about his life back home, where everyone was waiting for something better to come along before quitting their dead-end jobs, mismatched relationships, and boring social circles. He didn't just want Nila, he wanted all of this. But he knew it would need a miracle for this to happen.

Before the feast, Ranga and his two friends, who were considered to be the guiding light for the village, started the prayers. The feast started with a few people coming out to the centre and welcoming Adi. Ranga spoke about Adi, which took the villagers by surprise as Ranga was a man of few words.

The feast continued and people came to Adi, thanking him for the visit and also taking photographs with him. Finally, it all came to an end when the music ended and people began to disperse slowly.

Adi was getting restless, as he knew that it would be his final moment with Nila. His restlessness was too obvious on his face and he could hardly do anything about it.

"It's time to say goodbye to Adi as he is leaving tomorrow. Nila, you spent a lot of time with Adi. Why don't you thank him for us?" said Ranga.

Nila was taken aback when she heard her name and had no clue of what to speak.

She walked slowly to the centre and composed herself first.

With a soft voice, she said, "Adi is a nice person. I first

saw him snoring in my forest tree in the middle of the night. He thought he had escaped a panther, which was actually one of our pigs!"

Everyone laughed in unison.

She continued, "He looked at everything in awe, be it me or our little houses. He loves nature and his independence, just like us. Although I was the one who was speaking more, it was he who taught me more with his questions. I don't know how to say this, but I felt being protected within my own forest."

Everyone was quiet as Nila continued to speak the way she always did, truthfully and with love.

"We have many visitors who have stayed longer, but today I somehow feel responsible towards Adi. He needs to be happy always and we must ensure his happiness, considering the fact that he is going back to his life which he wanted to escape from. I just can't thank him enough for coming, and I feel there is a long way to go before he bids us goodbye."

There was complete silence after this talk. As everyone knew Nila personally, they wanted to protect her, no matter what her intentions were with the talk.

They continued to remain calm, trying not to interpret the talk unless she declared anything openly.

Ranga too was a mute witness.

He felt some inherent peace and remained calm for some time. Looking at Adi he said, "Adi, your final words before you start on your way tomorrow."

Adi was still trying to decipher Nila's words when he was called for the talk. He walked slowly, looking at Nila and the eager villagers who were expecting something different from him.

He knew that everything would end there with this

talk. He may just say goodbye and let this all disappear like a dream, or he could have one final try to make this dream become a reality.

"Good evening everybody. As you know, I was a traveller, visiting places trying to understand me with some self-centered motivation. It's like something out of the world would come and enlighten me! But nothing happened till yesterday. And today, I stand enlightened before you. I was thinking success was happiness... But you people taught me that happiness is a success."

Adi looked at everyone around him earnestly, and continued speaking into the still silence.

"For the first time in my life, I saw people anxious to help a stranger whom they have not seen or heard of before. I have to tell you all that I am an orphan. I lost my parents very early in my life. I was devoid of love for a very long time, which made me an expert in seeing it from very far. The peace your eyes expressed on seeing me alive yesterday made me believe in love more than ever."

Adi paused a second trying to control himself.

He continued "I could have thanked you all, and continued on my journey but I know this journey of mine is ending right here, and if it doesn't, then it's not my journey. Yesterday night, I accidentally ended up at Nila's tree house where she was sleeping peacefully. I was witnessing her sleep with a smile. And believe me... That was the best conversation I have ever had in my life. This one day made me realize how important I was through her eyes."

"Her life and love are infectious, and who better to authorize it than you people? She speaks with everything, she smiles at everything and she relates to everything."

He cleared his throat slightly.

"I know it might be too much to ask her all for myself, but I know it's not me getting her, but it will be she who will be letting me be a part of her wonderful world, which includes you lovely people too.

He chose his words carefully. "This is my last chance to propose to her and even if she says no, her memories will enrich my life forever."

Adi noticed that Nila was unable to control her tears, and was hiding behind the tree.

With his heart pounding, he looked longingly at Nila and said, "Nila, I know I just met you yesterday. But I don't have anybody in this world except you now. I was so anxious to propose to you in person, but now I am left with no other choice but to do it in front of the whole village. I want to be a part of your life Nila. Will you marry me?"

Nila was still silent, and so was everyone else. Ranga called out to Nila and said, "No matter what happens, you shall remain always ours and this forest will be your first home. Say yes if you want to marry him, the rest will be taken care of by love."

Nila said a yes with a teary smile. The whole crowd went berserk and the music started once again. This time, they had no intentions of stopping until the sun came out in the mountain village.

Adi sat down heavily, his heart still thumping like crazy. He closed his eyes, took a deep breath and smiled, with tears rolling down his face.

✦✦✦

Time Alone Heals Life

(The Search For The Past)

Adi spent more than a day travelling on a train to reach the only town that had the bus service to Nila's village. He was one of the early passengers to board the bus, and as always the conductor waited for the seats to be filled before blowing his whistle.

This was Adi's second trip after his accident. Last time, he had come in search of Nila just after his discharge from the hospital.

Sitting on the bus, he was looking at the passengers boarding it. They were all simple people, with no mystery surrounding their existence. Some of them recognized Adi and saluted him, to which he reciprocated by an acknowledging smile.

He saw the 'Woman Missing' poster of Nila still stuck at a roadside shop. He had pasted that himself during his previous visit.

He contemplated staying in the village for some more time to make sure he would get all possible clues, in addition to Nila's diary, which could help him in his search.

The bus started after nearly two hours and accommodated the last minute passengers who were ready to travel standing in the bus, for half the ticket price without getting one.

Boarding continued throughout the journey, as people stopped the bus at various points just by standing in front it with their families. The slow journey was not a concern for any of the passengers, as they knew it was their quickest way of commute, no matter how delayed it got.

The trip which was supposed to be completed in 6 hours took 10 whole hours till the engines were switched off in front of Lal's tea shop.

The bus was almost empty when it reached its destination. And if not for Adi and a couple of old men, the bus would have skipped its final stop, disappointing those who were looking forward to their onward trip to the city from the village.

Lal's eyes brightened on seeing Adi and he insisted on carrying Adi's luggage till his shop. He started to prepare coffee for Adi and the others who were lined up at his shop.

Adi was reminded of his first trip to the mountains and the subsequent events which started from Lal's tea shop. He chatted for a while with Lal and left for the village as the bus started its return journey.

***

Adi reached the village in the early hours of the day and still found the place busy with people engaging in some activity or the other. He knew that the people of the village sleep by dusk, and wake up before dawn, utilizing the maximum sunlight of the daytime.

The lack of electricity was a blessing in disguise. Interestingly, nobody owned a watch or phone, which subtracted the obvious tensions and added meaning to their simple life.

A few villagers noticed Adi at a distance, and rushed towards him barefoot, eager to inquire about Nila. He could hardly answer them, and just shook his head, disappointing them.

He saw Ranga calling him, seated in front of his house.

"How are you?" Ranga enquired in a concerned tone, looking at Adi's condition.

"Just alive, sir. Can't say anything more," Adi replied. "Police are yet to find any lead and my memory recall is still zero. I feel powerless..."

Ranga replied patiently, "Stay here for some time. Get stronger first. This is your family, and we will work out something together."

He asked Adi to get some sleep, and walked down the hill, remembering Nila with moist eyes.

As Adi entered the house, the scent of the place reminded him of Nila. The paintings, the clay structures, the decorations and everything about the house brought back memories of her, filling his heart with pain.

He couldn't sleep or even lie down. He rushed out to the forest in search of her diary.

***

Adi was restless. He couldn't focus on the flowers on the path, the green cover, the wind chimes and the art pieces which were all intact, untouched by any adversity. He started searching inside the tree house, which never had any storage space.

The house was empty except for some wooden carvings and some intelligent clay work. Adi tried taking apart the clay sculptures and the wooden walls, but it all ended up futile.

He searched the entrance, the whole tree, and even the garden around it but he couldn't find anything.

Dejected by this, he lied down on the grass, thinking about other possibilities, when two village men came in search of him with food. They joined the search for a couple of hours, but nothing materialized despite their good knowledge about the place.

Adi lost any hope of finding the diary at the tree house and decided to stay in the village for some more time to try checking out other possible places.

On the way back from the forest, Adi saw a group of ladies singing in chorus while cutting vegetables.

He proceeded towards them and sat there trying to start a conversation. Seeing Adi, they stopped singing and carried on with their jobs ignoring his presence.

He felt bad for interrupting their work and said, "Please don't mistake me, it's been a while since I have spoken to people, and I am getting terrified of my solitude"

The ladies, to whom he was invisible till then, were now concerned as they knew how Adi had been before.

They started a random conversation, trying to make him comfortable, which eventually led to discussions about his life in the city, as well as Nila's acceptance of the city after marriage.

Realising that these people were very fond of Nila, he asked, "Do you all miss Nila?"

The ladies suddenly became silent, wordlessly exposing their sadness.

Finally, an old woman from the group replied with a grim face. "Who doesn't? She was the life of the village. She beautified our lives and our village. We missed her after her marriage, and today she herself is missing.

"We all were furious with you at first. But we also knew your love for her... You are a good soul too. You are suffering as much as we are."

"I am sorry. I am angry at myself. But given my condition, I am just a vegetable." Adi said, understanding her agony.

He conversed with them for a while, and helped them in their work, ignoring their resistance. He felt that these ladies favoured the simple pleasures of life altogether, over the more rewarding and difficult things the city folks chase after.

He was amused by the effort and time taken to prepare every little thing on the dinner table, whereas even a thirty-minute wait for a pizza looked like an eternity in the city.

Adi felt a slight sense of peace that night, after spending time with the ladies and their families over dinner. He decided to visit every home the next day and try to speak to the people there.

He thought Nila might be have been close to someone out there who might give him some clue in his search.

He also had a hearty conversation with Ranga that night and felt like he had returned home after protracted weeks of solitude.

***

The next day, Adi woke up early to find Ranga fully ready, waiting for his counterparts to discuss the illegal logging activities in the forest with the authorities in the city.

"Adi, I am leaving to the city today and will be back by tomorrow. If you need anything please speak to Lal. I told him to be at the village today."

Adi acknowledged him and decided to get ready as well, to visit every house in the village and keep himself busy, rather than ruining himself with sadness and solitude. He started visiting houses and discussed with the families about

Nila and things they noticed when he and Nila had arrived at the village as a couple after their marriage.

Although the discussions didn't help him much in his search, they helped him get an insight into people's lives and their values.

He noticed that the people of the village managed their wants so naturally – as evident from the fewer possessions they owned.

These people lived as if they had realized that present is all they had. Adi's interaction with them made him feel lighter and somehow brought solace to his aching soul.

As Adi was coming out of one of the houses, he noticed a senior forest ranger, who had come to the village for his regular inspection, approaching him inquisitively. He enquired about the reason for Adi's presence in the village and was shocked on hearing his tales.

The talk which had begun as an inquiry slowly turned into a concerned conversation, and then into a friendly chat where both enjoyed each other's company.

Lal interrupted their chat with hot tea that both the men appreciated on that freezing morning.

Sipping his tea, Adi asked, "Sir, I was wondering if people here ever wanted to live in the city with all its comforts, or had they made peace with the village?"

"It's not that they don't know about the city life. Some of them have even left the village to settle down in the city. But most of them return here. The city life is tough and demanding, making it hard for them to enjoy what they do, whereas here they work together and never scheme against each other." The Ranger replied.

"But again, what makes people happy here? I mean… There is no television, no mobile, and no other source of entertainment as such. But I don't see anybody fretting over it."

The Ranger smiled. "Well, I have 30 years of service... And believe me, with my experience over these years, I have been happier in the forest than in the city. The so-called entertainment sources like television, cinema or even newspapers are addictions, just like cigarettes and drinks. The world remains the same before and after its consumption. We just assume that something important is happening during its consumption.

Adi couldn't help but wonder how simply the ranger had articulated quite a deep thought.

"I wish these villagers continue to teach this way of living to their future generations as well," Adi said, finishing his tea.

"Good living can't be taught, Aditya. It can only be shown by example."

With those parting words, the ranger excused himself, as he had to inspect a few more locations that day.

Adi sat there for a while, looking at the little houses on the beautiful terrain, and related it to the ranger's words, which made more sense now. He got up with a sigh and continued visiting other houses. In the very next house he went to, he came across a little girl named Venba who was delighted to see Adi in her house.

She loved speaking to Adi and started playing with him.

"She acts as if she knows me already!" Adi said to Venba's mother.

"Of course, she does. She was the one accompanying you and Nila all the while during your visit here after the marriage. You probably don't remember it, but she does!" the mother replied.

Adi felt puzzled. Hearing these words brought out his hitherto dormant helplessness to the fore. He realised that recently, he could have known a lot of new people.

He could have achieved a lot of things and could have created a bunch of memories but all of it had been wiped out. And today he was living in the present, having skipped over his recent memories.

He knelt down near Venba. "What did we do the last time when we met, sweetheart?"

Venba thought for a moment. "We made a toy together, with Nila, at the house on the tree."

Stunned, Adi asked again, "What did we make?"

"Animal toy with a round tail," she answered, with details this time.

"Can you show me if I take you there?" he asked, expecting something from it.

Venba nodded. Adi carried the little girl on his shoulders and started walking towards the woods. He took her to the tree house, the garden, the pond, and the space around it.

But she couldn't recognize anything like the toy she remembered making. After multiple trips around the area, Adi was losing any hopes of finding it.

He didn't want to disturb the little girl anymore, so he returned to the village, devoid of all the peace he had acquired over the day.

***

Adi was running out of the confidence that he had had while entering the village, and this was making his stay more difficult. Restless, he decided to go back to the city. He started packing his bag in haste when Ranga entered the house.

He asked, "Are you leaving?"

"Yes, sir. I am finding it hard to stay here. Moreover, I couldn't find what I came for..."

"Wait, don't be in haste. Sometimes you need a break to start things afresh. Or else you will get stuck in this relentless misery..."

Adi continued to listen wordlessly.

"I have instructed Lal to take you to the town tomorrow, and spend the day there."

Adi crossed his arms. "Sir, don't mistake me, but I don't feel like doing anything at this point."

Ranga, however, persisted. "As I said, a break can be helpful. Just be there without any apprehensions, and spend some time with the people around. Nila never missed the Wednesday market. It was her favourite time of the week."

Adi couldn't deny the request anymore and acknowledged Ranga's words by pausing his packing. He gently moved out of the house and wandered aimlessly around the forest till the darkness restricted him to sit on the rock where Ranga spent most of his mornings, overlooking the village.

The rock was like a time capsule for Adi, where the entire evening felt like a couple of minutes as he kept on looking at the houses, the people moving around them, and also the majestic forest which would probably feel protected by these simple people living their uncomplicated lives.

***

The next day, Adi was woken up by Lal who was in a white attire that he wore every time he visited the town.

He had borrowed a motorcycle from the neighbourhood for the trip, hoping that Adi would like to drive it through the mountains.

Adi could see the excitement in Lal's face as he opened up his tea shop to show Adi the bike. It was old but repainted all in black, marginally resembling Lal's excitement in his white attire.

Adi started the bike, with Lal riding pillion, holding some bags and a can of petrol. The bike, assisted by the downhill gravity, was still taking its time to manoeuver through the hills, thereby making sure that they didn't miss out any of nature's beauty on the way.

Lal requested Adi to stop the bike every now and then, on the pretext of a tea break or a loo break, just to make sure that the bike didn't heat up and got enough breaks, as per its owner's sincere advice.

After a long journey, they entered a village which had a small pond at its entrance.

As per Lal's suggestion, Adi parked the bike beside the lake and as he moved on, he noticed a series of shops on the other side of the pond.

This was when he realized that he was already in the town, which now looked way different compared to his memories of it. Lal pointed out the shops which constituted the Wednesday market and started walking towards it.

From nearby, Adi felt the market was bigger than how it appeared from a distance. It was essentially a primitive version of a modern mall with all the things needed for day-to-day living packed within few hundred meters of a noisy crowded place. Lal was already inside the market, which left Adi with no choice but to enter it as well.

"This is the only time of the week when we need money," Lal said.

Adi matched his fast pace, trying to escape the loud zone.

“This is not the regular market, its Wednesday market,” Lal said as if he was trying to make a point to Adi. “Vendors from all the nearby villages visit this place to put their shops. In addition to this, there are also separate markets for pulses, vegetables, and cattle.”

Adi was shaking his head all the way, just to make sure he reciprocated coherently to Lal’s talks. He did not want to offend Lal by ignoring him blatantly.

Adi realised that he could not escape the noise, as the shops kept spreading, with the incoming crowd adding to the chaos.

He noticed that there were bargains everywhere, and when he lent his ear to a couple of them, he felt it was very trivial – easily avoidable.

“Nila loves being here. She took me here a couple of times in the same bike we drove today,” Lal said.

Adi imagined Nila riding the bike. And his face lit up with a smile.

“If you have something to buy, please proceed. I shall wait near the parking spot,” Adi said, trying to escape the place.

“Don’t you want to see the other shops? There are many more…”

“No, it’s alright. Please don’t mistake me. I am not feeling well. Once you are done, we shall move on.”

“If you need something to drink, I will get it for you,” Lal offered.

Adi held Lal by his shoulders and said, “I am perfectly fine, Lal. Just finish your purchase and come back. I shall be waiting there”

As Lal walked backed to the shops, Adi escaped the market zone by taking a shortcut amidst one of the shops to an open space. He approached the pond and sat under a neem tree, whose roots served as his seat.

He kept looking at the excited kids in the market, as well as what looked like serious adult discussion but were probably not so. He noticed a vendor sitting near him, distributing newspapers to the incoming crowd with their ad posters pinned on them.

"Don't you deliver the newspapers to the people in the mountains?" Adi asked him.

"No, sir. It's a waste of time. First of all, it's difficult to reach them. And secondly, I don't think we can make much money out of it. Forget us… Even the letters are not delivered there," the vendor replied.

Adi acknowledged him and got one newspaper for himself. He was going through it when he saw that Lal was already in front of him with a cold drink bottle.

Adi smiled and took the bottle from him after giving it a second look. "What's the next move?"

"Ranga Sir instructed me to show you the market, take you around the town, and end the trip with a movie."

Adi took a deep breath, "Seriously?"

"Yes, sir," Lal replied with a sincere face.

After filling petrol, Adi started the bike to ride across the town as well as the market, as Lal kept insisting. During the course of the drive, Adi was looking at the vintage buildings, unique houses and the people who were looking back at him curiously, seated in front of their houses.

The drive somehow rekindled Adi's curiosity about the place and its people once again. Although he hadn't been keen on this trip–his priorities were different, and in fact, serious – he was subconsciously gelling with the environment of the simple small town.

His slow drive got slower and eventually stopped in front of a movie theatre, which resembled a suburban warehouse.

Adi saw the movie poster pasted outside the theatre and smiled. The movie had come out decades ago – it was older than him. As Adi was parking his bike, he noticed that Lal was sprinting towards the empty ticket counter just to make sure he didn't lose out on one.

"It's such an old movie, why do you want to watch it?" Adi asked as he joined Lal on his way towards the theatre.

"Have you seen this movie, sir?" asked Lal in return.

"Well, not really."

"Then you must watch it, sir. You will love the movie, especially the fighting scenes."

Adi didn't speak a word more as he sat on one of the premium segment seats – which were vintage wooden benches – neatly arranged behind the sand floor which happened to be the only other ticket option.

"Has Nila been here before?" Adi asked.

"Every Wednesday, unfailingly. She gets glued to the screen."

"I know," Adi said to himself, as he started watching the movie with Lal who was apparently becoming a teenager when the titles appeared on the screen.

Adi looked at the crowd. They were cheering every time they saw their hero on the screen. He could understand the infectious vibe of the place. He wondered if these people really prefer living this way. Sometimes, knowing nothing and living simply is better than knowing a lot and living a distant dream.

***

Adi's hiatus at the village was peaceful, despite not turning out the way he wanted. Everyone at the village empathized with him and tried to comfort him in all possible ways. With a whole village of well-wishers, he felt like he had a family there. This must be the feeling Nila would have had, he thought.

He was born somewhere, raised somewhere else, and now he shared a good relationship with people high up in the mountains, to whom he had been a stranger a few years ago.

He felt happy that this unique life was destined for him, and nothing about it would change.

Adi would always be welcome there, as a friend.

He decided to leave the village the next day, and continue with his search in the city. He conveyed it to Ranga, who accepted it this time, understanding that it was the way forward for Adi.

Adi had to catch the 3:00 AM bus, so he decided to leave the village without disturbing anyone. When he got ready and walked out, he saw the whole village waiting outside to bid him goodbye. Adi couldn't believe the loving gesture of these simple people and started thanking them one by one until he got emotional, and was unable to talk anymore.

His throat was choking with sadness and he burst into tears which had been mounting within him for a long time.

He felt that he had betrayed them by losing their Nila, but they were gracious enough not only to forgive him but also to take care of him just like he was one among them.

Adi drank the water someone offered to him, rubbed his tears, and said "My life was different until I met Nila. Today, this village, this forest, these mountains, these houses, and you people are all that I have. I came here searching for Nila like a nomad, but instead, I found the place where I belong, where I can cry, and where I will die. Wait for me. I will bring back Nila soon."

Ranga, who heard Adi, hugged him, and said, "Those were almost the same words you had expressed before when you felt you belonged here. But today you don't remember it. You have relived the same life but without Nila this time. We're glad you visited us, Adi. We are with you."

***

Adi reached home exhausted. He missed the village and wished he had settled there after his marriage. Then nothing bad could have ever happened. His house brought back the shallow feeling, which he tried to overcome by binging on black coffee.

He didn't want to let go of the thoughts of the village and its people.

His happiness depended on his surroundings, and the proof was the contentment he had felt in the village.

He took his coffee and walked towards the balcony, surprised to see the birds still visiting it. Trying to shift the cup to the other hand, he slipped on a wet patch on the floor, and fell on his stomach, spilling the coffee all over the place.

Annoyed, he sat back, cleaning the coffee on his hand when he noticed the clay structure at the centre of the balcony, which used to be a lush lawn. It was a handcrafted clay piece of an animal with its tail like a pig. Adi felt cold. He instantly knew that this was the toy the little girl had been speaking about.

It has been there all this while, but it was only now that it had gained his attention. He didn't remember making it with Nila, but he kind of knew it to be a half panther and half pig structure.

He smiled at it and noted a slot made in its bottom. He inserted his hands and felt the diary hidden inside. His hands shivered as he took out the diary. He kissed it, smelt it and rubbed his cheeks on it, taking a deep breath.

***

The handwritten words on the diary made Adi emotional. He started to live inside Nila's head for a while and started seeing her world with every page she had written. It helped him think like Nila, which he wanted badly.

Nila had spoken to him about her diary where she would write about her plans for tomorrow rather than her experience of today. She would paint her colourful imagination into it and eventually live way better than that.

He smiled when he read about her decision to pour water on a tree which wasn't receiving any direct rainfall, and then to watch the water trickle from it.

Adi's love and longing for Nila increased with every page he turned. He realized she was a pure diamond because of her courage to present a candid version of herself to the world. She wrote only one thing at a time, just the way she lived her life.

She would find happiness in something as simple as sitting, sipping water or just listening to music, and doing nothing else. He was wondering how such a girl could say yes to a lazy and a stupid man like him for marriage.

Adi was approaching the end of the diary, but he couldn't get any clue that would help him find Nila. He was in the final few pages when he found the name Raj Purniman, about whom she had spoken of highly.

She had wished to attend the escape programme run by Raj Purniman, along with Adi, and she had also mentioned that Adi needed that, and it might help him begin to see life differently.

"Raj Purniman. Have I heard this name before?" Adi wondered.

✦✦✦

The Future Starts Today

"Relax, and tell me the first thought that comes to your mind," Adi said, removing the blinds from Nila's eyes.

Standing at the entrance, she felt the cool breeze rushing from the open windows. "Beautiful," she said, opening her eyes to the sunlight radiating across the rooms of their new house.

She walked around excitedly and glanced out of the window. "Don't you think it's a bit high?" she asked. Their house was on the 18th floor of the building.

"Well, I think your house at the mountain was higher than this," he smiled, walking towards the balcony. Nila followed him eagerly.

"Can we get a swing here?" she asked.

"Sure, requirement noted. I am looking for more ideas from you."

Nila checked out the nearby balcony spaces excitedly, "Can we grow plants here?"

"Why not? I can get you a lawn here, just need a nod from you," Adi grinned, sensing her joy.

"That will be wonderful Adi. By the way, why doesn't anybody leave water for the birds?" she asked, trying to see all the balcony spaces visible.

Adi nodded. He looked out at the city and shouted, "Everybody out there, spare a moment, the Forest Queen has officially taken over, but don't worry, you are in safe hands now."

Nila approached him with a smile, held his hands, and looked at the busy people moving around, near the main gate. Her face slowly lost its colour.

"Missing home?" he asked.

"No, it's not that. Did you notice that no one smiled at us when we entered the building, not even in the lift?"

"What? Why should they?" he asked, a bit perplexed.

"Why not Adi? We are going to live here… as their neighbours. And even if we don't, what's wrong with a little smile?"

He brought her closer to him, and said, "It's a different world out here, Nila. Don't compare your beautiful village to this. But yes, we have to live here and I'm sure we will create our own awesome world here."

She smiled and hugged him tightly already feeling excited about what the place held in store for them.

"So, what else do you want to buy?" he asked.

"Some pots and plants, nothing much."

"I mean for the inside of the house," he said, still hugging her.

"What do you mean inside the house?" she asked, coming out of the hug this time.

"Utilities and stuff…, I mean things we need to live! Things that will make this our home," he exclaimed, unable to believe that he was explaining it.

"Like what?"

"Are you kidding me?" he asked, genuinely surprised.

"Well, I don't want to load our house, Adi. If there's anything important, I can get it from my village," she said with a serious face.

Adi was taken aback by the reply. He looked contemplatively at her. "That's so thoughtful of you Nila... By the way, what do you get from your village, apart from honey bottles and Lal's coffee powder?"

She stared at Adi for a second and laughed out loud, giving a friendly punch on his cheek. They both continued chatting in the balcony, with freshly brewed coffee in their hands.

"There is something which I wouldn't compromise on buying," Adi said, sipping his coffee.

"What is that?" she enquired keenly.

"A nice bed. You know, an average man spends one-third of his life on his bed and I am well above average. I spend my life on it, so I am not taking any chances there."

Nila gave a mischievous wink. "I still think we can sleep on the floor, you know. It's good for our health."

"Well, in that case, you must know that bed is a multipurpose tool. You can do more stuff on it. Not just sleeping. You know what I mean by more stuff, don't you?"

"Not really," she said shyly, blushing crimson and hiding her smile.

Adi didn't reply, but couldn't resist smiling which eventually turned into laughter.

"What?" Nila asked, joining the laughter without reason.

"Where do your mountain people do that important stuff? Don't they get hurt doing stuff?" he asked, and started running only to be pulled back by Nila who was delivering stronger punches this time.

“Are you sure the movie is a good idea?” asked Nila.

“I think so. Why are you asking this? Aren’t you interested?” Adi asked locking the doors.

“It’s not that… But I feel I need some more time to get used to all of this!”

“Don’t complicate things Nila. Anyway, I am with you through this.”

She nodded and looked at the hallway of the corridor. “So, do you know any of our neighbours?”

“Well not really,” Adi said, walking past her. “There are three other flats in this floor, excluding ours. One is under renovation, one is vacant, and the final one is rented to a family of a mother and a child.”

“Can we meet them?” Nila asked impulsively.

“Sure, but not now. We are already late if we factor in the traffic that would be out there.”

They were lucky not to have to wait for the lift, and they swiftly made their way to their car. Adi helped Nila with her seatbelts and decided to speed up so they could escape the peak time traffic than getting tormented by it.

During the course of the drive, he was detailing about all the landmark destinations on the way, which eventually became too much information for her to assimilate.

As Adi was about to take a U-turn, he noticed an auto approaching him fast in the opposite direction, missing a collision by a whisker. Both the vehicles came to an abrupt halt. Adi was furious about the auto driver’s carelessness. But he tried to remain calm, as he didn’t want Nila to be disturbed. The auto driver, however, walked towards Adi and started abusing him badly. Adi’s frustration peaked. He raised his middle finger and continued driving ahead.

Adi knew that Nila would have been disturbed by the course of events, and tried to console her, only to find her crying silently. He parked the car safely in a side lane and started speaking to her.

"Did you realize that it was his mistake?" he asked patiently.

Nila nodded mutely.

"You must have also realized that he was an arrogant chap who refused to accept it, and instead started shouting at me."

She nodded again.

"So tell me Nila, what was I supposed to do?"

"Nothing," she said, wiping her tears. "I couldn't tolerate so much anger, nor the idea of anybody hurting you, Adi!"

Adi held her hands. "Don't worry, Nila. I am sure that the auto driver must have picked up another fight by now. He's the one with problems, not us. Good people like us must be stronger. And stay above all this."

In response, Nila smiled at Adi and kissed his hands as the car cruised ahead on its way.

Adi asked Nila to wait at the entrance of the mall until he parked the car. After finding a parking space, he hurried towards Nila. She was still standing at the same place where he had dropped her, unable to cross the road against the outgoing cars from parking. He watched her for some more time and realized that she couldn't discern the oncoming vehicles' speed. She was not used to them in their village.

He rushed to Nila and guided her into the mall.

"This is a really big place!" She said, looking at the mall's enormity.

"So, you like the city finally?" he asked.

"It's good. But not as good as the city near my place."

"Okaayyy!" He said, stretching the syllables. He had visited the city which Nila was referring to. "So, you call that a city too?"

She gave a concerned look at him, and asked, "Why not?"

"No, I was just curious. I didn't know if a place with a tea shop and a vegetable market qualifies to be a city as well..." he said, with a serious face.

Nila put her hands on her hips and said, "Really?"

"Relax, I was just kidding!" Adi smiled. "I know it has to be a city, it had that bus stop shade made of dried palm leaves... Forward thinking, I must say."

Nila chuckled at the joke, gently hitting him on his shoulders as they approached the ticket counter.

"Did you notice, those guys were smiling at me as they crossed by?" Adi asked.

"Not just them, but a lot more people... I was smiling at them too."

Adi instantly understood what was happening. "Looks like someone finally felt welcome!"

Nila smiled back innocently, much to his delight.

Eventually, they were at the ticket counter, staring at houseful signs. He saw that most of the movies were full, and the only one that had tickets was better left alone. He conveyed it to Nila, but she was excited to see any movie available.

Adi entered the movie hall and found it to be empty, in spite of it being a weekend night. "Why do they screen it anyway?" he asked himself.

As they got seated, he noted that they were not alone. There were some busy people, immersed in love, settled in the corners.

He started hearing snoring sounds even before the titles were displayed, and this set the tone for his movie watching experience.

He fell asleep too, soon after the hero's entry, and then was woken up once in a while by the angry villain, only to be put back to rest by the marathon action sequences.

During this entire experience, he realized that Nila was glued to the screens, unperturbed by the fact that everyone in the movie was excited by almost everything in the movie.

Adi knew that he had a long night ahead, and completed half of his night's sleep at the theatre. As they walked out, Nila asked, "Do you think people like Kaza exist? How can one be so ruthless?"

Thankfully the only thing Adi knew about the movie was the Villain's name – Kaza. He said, "Yeah, I know. It's the director's vision, though!"

He was just hoping Nila didn't ask him anymore, and muttered to himself, "It's not Kaza, but the director who was ruthless. He was the one butchering logic mercilessly, and didn't even let it die in peace!"

***

As a part of his entrepreneur journey, Adi had decided to recruit people with a placement drive which was being organized in the neighbouring district. He had decided to take the help of his best friend, Qadir who, incidentally, was a seasoned entrepreneur as well.

"So when will you be back?" asked Nila.

"Maybe two- or three-days max. What do you say, Qadir?" Adi asked Qadir who was at his place, with his wife Mehar.

"Yeah, anyway I have to come back by then. Or my employees will sell my company!" Qadir said, laughing at his own joke.

"Don't worry, Nila. We're finally getting our own shopping time." Mehar grinned, winking at Nila.

"Someone is going to be bankrupt even before starting the company!" Qadir laughed heartily.

"Not at all! Nila hates shopping, and I love her for that." Adi smiled at Nila.

"Some people are really lucky…" Qadir said, with an exaggerated funny shrug. "By the way, leaving Mehar and Nila together is the best idea we've ever had. No matter who influences who, I have nothing to lose!" Qadir laughed again at Mehar's faux furious look.

"You can't joke beyond wives and marriage, Qadir!" Mehar said and turned to Adi. "How come you got married, Adi? You said you weren't ready for that!"

As Adi was about to answer, Qadir interrupted, "Good God! He didn't wait to get everything right before finding a partner. The population would have died off long ago then!"

The jokes continued for a while, after which they assembled for breakfast. Nila was getting emotional with every passing minute. She started missing Adi already. Adi was aware of Nila's state of mind, but couldn't do much in front of the guests.

As Adi was about to leave the house, he looked at Mehar. "You guys take care… By the way, I must say that Nila is kind of soft… I mean… Sensitive,"

Before he could complete, Mehar interrupted.

"Oh, really? I love soft people, they taste great. Qadir, would you like to try it as well?" She asked with a serious face, pulling Adi's leg.

Adi gave an embarrassed look as everyone joined the laughter, including Nila.

He waved a bye to Nila and told Mehar, "Stay away from Qadir. You are getting seriously funny!"

***

Adi and Qadir were the first company in the placement drive process and were amazed at the huge turnout of participants. The arrangement, however, was bad and cumbersome, leading to lots of delays, making the event extend by another day.

Adi found it hard to identify the right candidate and pushed his luck till the last day. But he had to return empty-handed, but loaded with the wisdom about the present day job market.

"Most of these guys belong to our age group, and yet, they could hardly get their basics right," Adi said on their way back home.

"Well, they are trained for the exams, Adi, and not for life," replied Qadir

"But still, Qadir..." Adi hesitated.

But Qadir interrupted abruptly saying, "Ignorance is a big subject to discuss on a drive. Let's leave it at that."

"What about my company then?"

"We will get freshers, train them, and tune them to our needs."

"Not sure if I can trust them," Adi said with concern.

"Adi, please don't feel the need to be the absolute best. Start trusting others, or else you must do everything by yourself. Is that possible?"

Adi acknowledged Qadir's words as they halted to get some coffee before driving into the night. Over coffee, Qadir asked, "So, how's life after marriage?"

"Well, never better. I don't know how to express, but I feel extra conscious of everything, and a bit responsible too."

"Wow, that's deep. Anyway, if you are happy, I am happy"

"I know," Adi acknowledged the statement with a smile.

"Well, stop by some jewellery shop on the way if you come across one," Qadir said.

"Why?"

"Well, it's my wedding anniversary tomorrow. I need to renew my marriage for yet another year."

***

Adi knocked on the door, hiding flowers behind his hands, and a smile behind his eyes. This was the first time he had stayed away from Nila after marriage, and he couldn't wait to get a glimpse of her. He pressed the calling bell again restlessly.

Nila opened the door slowly and closed it from behind. She hugged Adi and kissed him as her eyes got moist with happiness. Adi kissed her back and felt at home.

Nila took a black cloth from her skirt pocket and blindfolded him, signalling him not to speak anything. Once blindfolded she took him directly into the bedroom.

She made him stand at the door and removed the blindfold. Adi opened his eyes to a pleasant surprise. He was looking at something which hardly resembled his previous bedroom. Nila had changed its decor and made it look almost similar to her tree house. The wallpapers resembled wood and accessories were similar to the ones at her tree house.

"Are you serious?" he asked, totally taken aback by the surprise. "Just three days and you did all of this?!"

She gave an engaging smile. "I missed you and my mountains, so I thought of creating a little tree house in our city house."

Adi felt immensely happy knowing it won't be the same bedroom anymore. He walked around the house. So much has changed – especially the balcony, which looked a lot greener now. Predominantly, he was happy for Nila as she had started coming to terms with the changes in her life.

***

Adi was looking at the freshly made idlies with colourful chutneys all around, making it look like a moon surrounded by a rainbow. He took a bite of it and loved it thoroughly.

"Nila, trust me… This is not just an Idli but a piece of heaven on a plate," he said relishing the bite.

She sat next to him with hands on her cheek and asked, "Are you sure?"

"I am serious. You know, this is not the first time I am eating Idli, but believe me, it's simply awesome!"

"I think everyone makes Idli the same way," she replied, placing two more Idlies onto his plate.

He smiled at her reply, "I wish cooking was as simple as your reply Nila, but unfortunately it's not. It's actually about how you play with the raw materials and how much you involve yourself in the process. That makes all the difference. Food is not just the taste, it's the smell, look, warmth, feel, crispiness, softness, chewiness, shallowness and actually, it's more than sex if you can feel it."

Nila laughed loudly.

"I am serious, Nila," he said emphatically.

Trying to control her laughter, she came close to him and whispered into his ears, "Then you must sleep with one of these idlies tonight!"

Adi joined the laughter this time. They continued with their discussions at the balcony, with Adi holding his usual post breakfast tea.

"Well, if not for this android thing, I would have started a restaurant."

"Not a bad idea. Would you have allowed me to cook there?"

"Oh yes! You will be the chief cook. Having a cook who can't run away from you makes so much of difference! Actually, it's a huge business today, as people don't find time to cook for themselves even in a family."

"But I don't understand. Cooking for loved ones is a special feeling, why miss that?" She asked.

"Well, that's right. But they might compensate it by eating together, and that is love too. At the end of the day, love is about getting the hormones released by some way or other, isn't it?" he asked trying to pull her close.

"No, it is not. It's a deep mystical experience… And please, no hormone jokes again." She said, giving him a furious look.

"Oops, I forgot that hormones make you angry, too." He said, pulling her close again.

"I am not angry. I was just wondering if this is your idea of about love in the bed as well…"

Adi choked and coughed his tea out. He looked at the smiling Nila.

"Maybe I should try it right away," Adi exclaimed and stood up from the swing.

Seeing Adi approaching her, Nila couldn't stop laughing as she dodged and tried to escape him.

Adi started chasing her into the house, and they ended up on the bed, holding each other.

"What are you planning now?" she gasped.

"To check if my hormone levels are alright," he replied, removing his shirt in a hurry.

"Wait for me. I will be back in a sec," Nila said, and rushed out of the bedroom, annoying Adi who was in the last piece of his clothing.

Nila walked back with something in her hand. She came close to Adi and whispered, "She was unwilling at first, but I convinced her for just one time…"

She opened her hand to show the idly in her palms. Adi looked up at her with a mixture of laughter and exasperation as Nila tried to control her laughter.

"I won't let both of you escape today," he jumped on her, making an awesome threesome to start the day.

***

Adi started working on his company without formally launching it. It slowly became a small functional unit with people joining through referrals from Qadir.

Within no time, Adi's schedule got packed with customer meetings and programming codes. He tried accommodating Nila at his office, but it did more harm than good as space and time were constrained there.

Nila decided to stay back home, subtly understanding Adi's situation. In spite of Adi trying to compensate for his absence with utilities like television, it did no good to her, as she easily got bored with them over time.

She decided to meet her only neighbour, whose doors always remained closed.

She gave a lot of thought before knocking at her neighbour's house.

Just after a single gentle knock, a young lady opened it, delighted to find Nila there. She smiled at Nila and welcomed her in.

"I had wanted to meet you, too, but was a bit hesitant." The woman confessed.

"Oh, I see," said Nila, pleasantly surprised by her treatment.

"I am Meera. This is my girl, Pari." The woman said, pointing to a little girl sleeping on the bed.

"Oh, she's beautiful!" Nila smiled and introduced herself. "Does she go to school?"

"Well, actually, she is kind of different... She is a bit mentally challenged... And I'm here for her treatment," Meera replied, her voice breaking with the words.

Nila held Meera's hands, empathising with her. "How old is she?"

"She is six, but has the maturity of a two-year-old girl."

"That's like living an extended childhood," said Nila, taking Meera by surprise.

That was something Meera had never heard before.

Meera looked at Pari, whose eyes had become moist. "I am living here with Pari for the past one and a half years, all alone. I don't know about her, but I am dying every day out of depression and solitude."

"Not anymore. I am here," Nila said holding Meera's hands once again.

The discussion about their lives bonded them big time, when Pari woke up from her sleep and rushed to Meera after finding a stranger in her house. Meera pointed to the sweet box placed above the fridge, which Nila could bribe Pari with, to gain her friendship.

When Nila offered sweets, Pari grabbed two of them instantly. She looked at Nila for a while, smiled at her, and offered one to her.

Tears rolled down Nila's eyes. She was humbled by the beauty of that little soul. She kissed Pari, and said, "I have sweets at home. These are all for you!"

Nila developed a special bond with Pari within a couple of days, much to Meera's astonishment. Pari was a reserved child and would normally shy away from new people. It was the first time in her life that Meera had left Pari under someone else's supervision, and felt fine with it.

"You are a magic girl," said Meera, looking at Nila who was feeding Pari her lunch.

"Why?" Nila asked, quite surprised.

"I have never seen Pari so happy with a new person. That too so soon."

"It's not me. It is she who hooks me with her magic!"

"That speaks of your kindness Nila, but I know how hard it is."

"What are you talking about? I mean I seriously enjoy her company. There is no talk of obligating kindness here," said Nila, emphasising her point.

Meera smiled at Nila. "She is not normal, Nila. And you know that. She can hardly take care of herself. Then how can she entertain you?"

"Look at her," Nila said, pointing at Pari. "You give her a leaf and she keeps admiring it for hours. She loves things with her heart. What else can you ask for?"

"That's true… But being a mother to a special child is different, Nila… You won't be able to understand it."

Nila kept silent for a moment and answered back, "I don't know about being a mother, but surely I know what it is to be a kid…"

***

Meera had invited Nila to join her for Pari's annual day celebrations at school. Adi was invited too. But he had an important client visit that day, so he had to decline and ask Nila to go with Meera. However, he made all the arrangements for a safe and comfortable commute for them.

Nila and Meera gave final touches to Pari's costume, left her backstage with her teacher, and occupied the back seats in the auditorium the only ones vacant.

"I was informed that Raj Purniman is expected today," Meera said.

"Who is that?"

"Oh!" Meera replied, realizing that Nila had never been there before. "He is the founder of this place and a mystery man."

"Why is that?" Nila asked.

"That's a long story, but to keep it short, he lives his life by his own rules, and goes out of the way to help those in need," Meera said as she stood up for the prayers before the start of the event.

As the program started, Meera was so engrossed in the event that she forgot that the kids performing there were special children, until Pari entered the stage like an angel.

Meera found the atmosphere happy and overwhelming. She started crying uncontrollably when she saw Pari performing.

Nila hugged her, understanding the emotions she was going through.

"Do you think she can become normal like us, Nila?" Meera asked.

"Well, children are remarkably honest, until we teach them not to be," said a voice from behind them.

Meera turned back to see an old man smiling at her, and said, "Excuse me!"

"Well you are excused this time" he replied and sat near Meera. "So which of these kids is yours?"

Meera pointed out Pari, unable to refute the sharp personality of the old man.

"She is perfect. What is it that you want to change in her?" The Old Man asked.

Meera didn't say a word, as she wanted to avoid a discussion in first place.

The man smiled at Meera. "When man discovered mirror, he lost his soul. If your vision is based on the social mirror, then I am afraid your choices will be influenced by others, making life meaningless. For all I can see, your little girl's life is more meaningful than yours."

Meera felt like a sharp slap on her face. Finally, she managed to answer, "If she is happy then I am fine."

"Wrong again. She learns happiness from you. You can't teach it to her unless you live by it."

Meera was not embarrassed by the words this time but felt a sense of peace.

She asked him, "Sir, are you a visitor here?"

"Yes, but I started this as well."

"Raj Purniman?" Meera asked, excited, as realisation dawned.

"I can see a kid in your face too!" The man smiled.

Meera could not contain her excitement. "I can't say how much I am indebted to you and your school sir. I can never repay it."

"Well, it is not about repayment but if you want to do something, you can try volunteering here, and make some difference."

Meera paused. "I am leaving to America with Pari soon. My husband has been waiting for us for quite some time."

Raj Purniman acknowledged with a slow nod and looked at Nila with a smile. "How about you, young lady? Have you ever thought about volunteering?"

✦✦✦

The Universe Speaks If You Can Listen

Adi was at the Special Children's School office, seated in front of the principal. He had a strange sense of déjà vu in that room, but given his condition, he couldn't recall much.

The principal, Karl, was an American who had volunteered to serve the institution, after spending some time with Raj Purniman during his visit to India, on a spiritual quest. He listened to Adi in detail and sympathized with his condition.

"You just can't believe what life throws at you sometimes," Karl said, understanding Adi's situation.

"Sometimes I wish all this would be a nightmare which I would wake up from," Adi said.

He looked exhausted and feeble, with his unshaven beard and reddened eyes.

Karl could see the pain Adi was going through and related it to his personal loss a few years ago when he lost his only son to cancer.

"Aditya, how do you think Raj can help you?" he asked.

"I don't know sir. I don't have any idea. But he is the only clue I could get from Nila's diary. I am tired of thinking anymore, but I can't stop searching for her. I know she is waiting for me somewhere."

Karl remained calm for a while and said "I have joined this school as the Principal just a month ago, and will serve for a short while only. In fact, most of the people working here are volunteers, and they are here because of their conviction to help this noble cause. I don't know if you have heard about Dr. Raj Purniman, but I must tell you that he is the strangest, and strongest soul I have ever encountered."

"Can I meet him?" Adi asked anxiously.

"Well, not until he wishes to. Most of the volunteers here have met him by accident, or through some reference..."

"Sir, I want to meet him... just once, please!" Adi pleaded, his voice burdened by sorrow.

"Listen, Aditya, I understand your position. But even we don't get to meet Raj that easily. He's a wanderer, and his only way of communication is through his handwritten letters. He visits us very rarely. But he's frequently spotted at the escape programme, which we conduct every month..." Karl said.

Adi was saddened by Karl's words. He had expected to meet Dr. Raj Purniman at the earliest. "Do you have any idea where he lives?"

"I don't know... But to live alone is the fate of all great souls." Karl paused. "I strongly suggest you attend the escape programme. You might be lucky and get to meet him there."

Adi thought for a while, and with a sudden gush of energy, asked Karl, "Do you maintain any record of the people who attend this escape programme?"

"Yes, we do, but why are you asking that?"

"What if Nila and I had already attended it?" Adi asked, wanting to check the records immediately.

Karl was excited about this possibility, too, although they both were clueless about their next action even if they did find Nila's name in it.

After an hour of scanning through the names repeatedly, Adi couldn't find their names in the register.

"Are you sure there are no chances of skipping our names?" he asked, desperately.

"We are thorough and regular about this. You better fill this form and get enrolled in this programme starting tomorrow. It is a continuous programme, with some joining it, and some leaving it every day."

"But what is this programme about?" asked Adi, a bit frustrated.

"It's equivalent to therapy for people suffering from depression, stress, and terminal diseases."

"You mean it's not for normal people?" Adi asked again.

Karl smiled, "Just fill the form and hope to see Raj there."

***

Ever since he had woken up from the accident, Adi had forgotten how to sleep naturally. It was the exhaustion, and sometimes intoxication, that helped him sleep in the early hours of the day, leaving him dehydrated and dull for the next day, only to get the cycle repeated. He survived on the little naps he got while travelling. He was napping on his way to the escape programme, which was interrupted by the sudden brake of the cab driver.

He quickly realized that he was already near the hill where the escape programme was being conducted. It was the same hill that was visible from his office window, but it had never occurred to him to actually go there.

As Adi closed in on the hill, he saw a lady in a brown drape standing at the foothills, along with a young guy who was sitting on a rock beside her. Once out of the cab, he was welcomed by the lady, who introduced herself as Asha, and informed that she had been volunteering during the weekends.

She introduced Adi to the young guy, Kunal, a college student and also a participant in the programme.

“The roads on the hill are under maintenance, hence we couldn’t allow cars inside. I hope it won’t be a problem for you to climb the hills…” she inquired.

Adi nodded to show he could walk, and started walking uphill after glancing at Kunal, who looked pale and weak. The walk through the hill was nostalgic for Adi, as it reminded him of some beautiful memories of Nila’s village and also the times he had spent trekking with her.

The hill had been an elevated desert once, but ever since it was taken over by the school trust, it got a new life in the form of trees and plants spread evenly around it. It housed a small temple at the top, which was frequented by the locals at the beginning of every year to conduct rituals.

As they continued uphill, Asha looked at Kunal and asked him, “Are you alright?”

Kunal did not answer, but continued to walk, ignoring everything around.

Adi felt something was wrong with him. He asked Asha, “What happened to him?”

Asha hesitated a bit. Then she said in a low voice. “He tried to commit suicide by consuming poison.”

Adi was shocked. ”But why?”

“Love failure,” she whispered back, not wanting Kunal to hear her.

Adi just shook his head in disbelief. “At this age? Seriously?”

Asha nodded. “More than his love, it was his violent family that pushed him to his limit.”

Adi felt bad for Kunal. Later it occurred to him that only people with problems were expected there. Although that included him, it was for a different reason.

Asha received a phone call and she was asked to be at the foothills for guiding the next batch of incoming visitors. She excused herself, and requested Adi to proceed, and also to have an eye on Kunal.

As Adi continued to walk, he noticed that Kunal was feeling irritated with the walk.

"Did you eat something?" Adi asked him.

Kunal didn't reply but was diverted by Adi's question.

Adi opened his bag to take out a biscuit packet, which had been his staple diet off late and handed it over to Kunal.

Kunal refused initially, but Adi pushed it into his hands and continued to walk along.

"Why do you want to die?" Adi asked.

Kunal didn't respond and kept his head down. After a while, with his eyes still fixed to the ground, he said "Nobody likes me. No matter what I do, I end up as a failure. I just hate myself."

"So you decided to die?"

Annoyed by Adi's question, he said, "You won't understand. This is my life, day in and day out."

"Then help me understand!"

"Why should I?" Kunal asked, perturbed. "My life is like this game where everyone shoots at you from all directions. I just don't know where to go, or what to do."

Adi gave a soft smile which Kunal did not note.

"Well, if you keep fighting all the shooters around, you will never reach your destination. Try escaping them for a change."

Adi's talk, coupled with the creamy biscuit that reduced his hunger, helped Kunal to gain some perspective.

"I lost my parents very early in my life, and I grew up almost alone amidst my relatives, who were vying for my father's property. Early on in my life, I understood what solitude is, and very recently, understood what love is. Please don't think that people can't relate to you… I can, very well."

Adi said, understanding that Kunal was getting comfortable with him.

It took almost an hour for them to reach the top, which housed the temple as well as their lodging. Standing at the top of the hill, Adi looked down at the whole landscape of the city, with its parched water bodies. He felt he had trekked all this while to escape from his world to reach a place which was totally immune to all worldly worries.

"Nila must be somewhere there," he said to himself.

***

Adi saw a row of tents for the participants and there were few people who had arrived at the summit already. At the centre of the hill, there was a small temple – a construction with transparent hardened glass walls. It possessed just a unique stone in the middle, which resembled a porous sun disfigured by age and nature.

It was after a long time that Adi didn't feel depressed. He was lost in the curiosity of exploring the place, which had unique flora and construction that brought out the child in him. With its solar energy installations and water harvesting systems, it was self-sufficient, in addition to keeping the place greener, and comfortable for its visitors.

This place had been the only saving grace for some birds and animals, which otherwise might have disappeared from this part of the land.

As Adi was walking back to the centre, there was a call for the participants, asking them to assemble before the temple. He noticed that people with varied personalities were emerging from their tents. Asha was guiding them to a small naturally formed platform and informed that the meeting is only for the new participants. This reduced the group to a handful of people standing before her.

She noted down the names of the people at the gathering and informed them that their role was different from those already present at the hills, as most of them were volunteers staying for the weekend. She divided the participants into two batches of four each and called out Daya, who was the coordinator for the tasks.

"This is Daya. He will be the point of contact for all your needs" she said and gave the list to Daya. She added, "As you can see, you have been divided into two groups. Each group will be given a different task to begin with, which has to be executed individually. Once it is completed, the tasks will be interchanged among the groups."

"What are the tasks?" asked a lady participant.

"The tasks, or the programmes, as I would like to call it, are the graveyard programme and beggars programme."

Asha's talk was interrupted by a loud laugh from Agarwal, an obese middle-aged participant, who shouted, "Are you guys kidding here?"

"No, sir," Asha replied firmly. "As you know, it's a free programme, where people come to get better. We don't have any liberty to ridicule it. In the interest of others, we can't allow anyone else to ridicule it as well. So you are free to leave, sir!"

Agarwal was stunned by Asha's sharp remark and fell silent without even bothering to apologize. He murmured, "They can't even speak courteously, what else you expect them to teach?"

Adi remained a mute spectator, as he knew that he had nothing to do with the programme. All he wanted was a glimpse of Raj Purniman.

"Owing to the construction work on the roads, we intend to start the programme only from tomorrow. Feel free to explore the place, and don't hesitate to contact us for any assistance. Daya will guide you through the programme, and he shall hand over the communication in the form of letters from time to time. Hope you all have a pleasant and productive time here!" Asha said and got down from the platform.

As the people started dispersing to their allotted tents, Adi was anxiously making his way to meet Asha. She noticed and came towards him.

"Any problem?" she asked, concerned.

"I came here to meet Mr. Raj Purniman, and it's an emergency," he said.

Asha enquired about Adi's problem in detail and informed him that Raj Purniman was expected there that week. However, she could not give any assurance for that. On further discussion, she told that the best option for Adi would be to participate in the graveyard programme for which Raj Purniman was known to make an appearance.

Adi could not speak much. He realised that no one had proper information on Raj Purniman and his whereabouts. The man remained elusive and Adi's best chance to see him was to go to places where he was expected to come.

Daya directed Adi to his tent. Adi noticed that the members had already started socializing over cups of tea.

He saw Kunal sitting silently in a group that had the loud-mouthed Agarwal in the centre.

Adi found the tent adequate and well maintained, with essential amenities for a basic stay. He was going through some of the books placed there when he heard Daya calling him from outside. Daya was standing with a cup of tea and a pack of biscuits.

"I noticed that you have missed your tea, sir!"

Receiving the cup, Adi thanked him for the concern and thought of asking him about Raj Purniman.

"Well Daya, please listen to me clearly. I am not here for any therapy or counselling, I just need some information from Raj Purniman about my lost wife, which he may or may not know. Do you have any idea where I can find him?"

"No, sir. Dinner will be served by 8.00 PM outdoors, along with other activities for the participants. Please be there on time." Daya informed and left the spot.

Taken aback by the reply, Adi decided not to push anyone anymore on this. He hoped to meet Raj Purniman naturally during the course of the events. That was probably his only option. Other than that, Adi kept to himself. He avoided meeting people and often wandered about the hills aimlessly.

Once on a solitary walk, it occurred to him that the voice in his head, which he had been hearing for a long time, had become silent. He realized that wishing that things had turned out differently was just a great way to torture himself. This silence, although guilty, was a harmless and optimal solution for his current predicament.

He strolled on the little paths constructed for walking on the hills, which in turn bifurcated differently and curtailed into shady sitting spots – Adi assumed they were meditation spots. He was convinced that there could be no better place for meditation than this. It was an oasis amidst the concrete desert he was used to.

It became dark, but Adi never stopped walking. The solar lights fitted across the paths guided him in this journey, which finally ended up at the temple, where he saw Daya waiting for him with his dinner and a letter.

Adi received it from Daya, thanked him once again for the concern, and walked back into his tent.

Keeping the dinner aside, he opened the letter. It read:

Dear Participant,

Why so busy, when you know, finally, it all goes easily?

Why try catching the illusion of the future, which always makes you a loser?

Why push to have something, when you can always pretend anything?

Why forget your inevitable death, which you brought with your birth?

Why fear to die, when your life itself can be a lie?

Make your own grave, live with it, embrace the consciousness, and re-affirm your existence.

For all you know, the beauty of life begins with its death.

Happy Dying.

Raj Purniman.

***

Adi heard the birds chirping, and the leaves rustling loud enough to feel as if it was a jungle out there. He woke up to nature's music, and finally got a break from his morning headaches. He walked out of the tent and was welcomed by the cold breeze laced with the aroma of the tea which was being served. He took his cup and looked out at the city below, which was still peacefully asleep. He walked to one of those meditation points which had enticed him, and had his tea in nature's nest, amidst the company of squirrels and sparrows.

He had nearly finished his tea when he noticed a truck with cement bags arriving at the foot of the hills. He saw Daya inspecting the bags stacked in the truck.

"What are these for?" asked Vikas, one of the participants who belonged to the graveyard team.

"It's for the tombstone construction, sir. It shall be unloaded at the graveyard site, where you will be allotted places for construction," Daya replied.

"But why at a graveyard? Can't we do it here?"

"Sir, apart from construction of tombstone, the participants are expected to work in the graveyard, assisting the death ceremonies. That's the reason the location is fixed there."

"But there was no mention of this in the letter!" Vikas exclaimed.

"Sir, we shall leave in an hour. Please complete your breakfast, and be ready." Daya replied and moved on with his work, leaving Vikas gazing at him.

Adi was in no mood to hurry. He got himself another cup of tea and sat back to enjoy the experience once again. He compensated the time spent on tea by skipping his breakfast, just to be on time to board the van. The trip started with the graveyard team. They were busy discussing the activities that were conducted at the hill the night before. They ignored Adi's presence. He was just a mysterious stranger to them.

The drive down the hill was short but beautiful amidst the unique hill with its newly laid roads. The graveyard was situated a few kilometres away from the hill, and it was predominantly used by the villagers nearby. As the van approached the graveyard, Adi noticed that people had already assembled there for a funeral.

As Adi got down from the van, there was a noisy crowd with cries all over. Some of them were in deep grief, whereas some were in a hurry to finish the proceedings and move on. It was the first time Adi had visited a graveyard, and the scenes were making him restless. He walked out to a calmer place, where he saw Daya arranging bricks and marking the place where the tombstones were supposed to be constructed.

As Adi started to get a hang of that place, Daya left him alone, after giving all the instructions to be followed. Adi was also supposed to volunteer for the funeral ceremonies at the burial ground, in addition to the construction of his grave. He was reluctant to begin, especially with all the chaos around. However, as the day progressed, he started accepting work from the people who were approaching him for help, and slowly got busy with the funeral services.

Very soon, he was immune to the cries around him and started handling the dead bodies for the first time in his life. The first day of his training witnessed a total of four deaths, which included a newborn baby, and war veteran aged hundred. By the end of the day, the place became quiet, like the calm after a storm, and that was when all the volunteers started arranging things for the construction of their grave.

It became increasingly difficult for the volunteers to work, as exhaustion and darkness started to catch up. Daya came back with the van to pick them up. Seated in the van, Adi was thinking about all the deaths he had witnessed that day and felt they were too unfortunate to die so young, except for the war veteran.

The suicide of the young girl for failing in an exam worried him the worst. Her mother's cry was still haunting his ears. The death of different people for different reasons kept him wondering about his life. He was even amazed to see that some people were getting over it immediately, once the cremation of their loved ones was over.

As the van started going up the hills, he felt peace embracing him. Something inside him told him that he would find Nila soon.

Once he stepped out of the van, he heard loud noises near the tents. He turned and noticed that Mr. Agarwal was animatedly arguing, angry about the way he was treated during his task of begging. He also shouted at the facilities provided in the tent and was packing his bags, getting ready to leave the place immediately.

"Sir, will you leave before or after dinner?" Daya asked politely, explaining that he needed to give his inputs to the cook.

Mr. Agarwal, agitated with Daya's total indifference, replied, "Of course, after the dinner. What did you think?"

Adi laughed at this from a distance and started walking towards his tent when he noticed Kunal approaching him with an uncontrollable smile that Adi reciprocated.

"You're looking happy!" Adi exclaimed, feeling happy for Kunal.

"Believe me, I have never laughed this much before this day in my entire life," Kunal said, still unable to stop his laughter.

"What happened?" Adi asked.

With recurrent giggles, Kunal explained, "Well, today we were made to beg in front of a railway platform, with some ridiculous costumes they gave us to make us resemble beggars. The fun started when Mr. Agarwal wore the dress, in which he looked like a harassed Santa who had lost his sanity.

He could not even bear people looking down on him. He kept shouting at all the passengers and was lucky to be mistaken for a mentally disturbed beggar. It was very funny to see his shouts and the terrified people passing by. I laughed even at my own condition. I was sitting next to him, in that garbage costume, and was watching all this."

Adi laughed with Kunal, Mr. Agarwal's voice still humming in the background.

"I wish I was in your team!" Adi said. "So do you think the task is helping you?"

"I don't know. But after the initial hesitations, I found it easy. In fact, I felt superior in front of the busy crowds, who were always on their toes."

Adi smiled. "Really?"

"Yeah, I mean, there was definitely nothing to lose and nothing to prove. It's like… you are still you, yet invisible to others. It's a liberating feeling."

"I get that. Anyway, Mr. Agarwal is packing his bags. You might miss him tomorrow."

"Yeah, I know. He gets the 'Man of the Match in Drama' award for sure. But I don't think it should be a problem for me tomorrow, as I kind of know the place and the people already. While leaving today, I heard someone saying that there were some families living in the station, under the disguise of passengers, owing to poverty. I want to see them tomorrow."

Adi nodded, surprised to see the difference a single day had brought in Kunal.

"Can I get your group's task letter?" asked Kunal.

"Sure," replied Adi, and handed it over to him.

"This is our group's list," said Kunal, giving his task letter. "Our letter has no mention of the damaged sandals which we had to repair during the task."

***

Sitting on a bench that overlooked the city landscape, Adi opened the letter and read it under the light of the solar lamp.

Dear Volunteer

Why can't you live like yourself, when nature's creations teach it to you?

Why seek approval from the rest of the world, making you a stranger in your own world?

Why follow everyone's dreams when your soul screams for you to be original?

Why stick to a glittering past when even the present escapes your grasp so fast?

Why judge the pretentious world when those judgments keep everyone's lives on hold?

Dance in the rains, and quell the ego the world has painted on you. Start living away from judgments, and start practicing mindfulness of the only truth, the present.

Start begging, and you will see yourself the way nobody else will see. You will see others the way nobody tries to see.

You will see everything that nobody else can ever see.

Happy Begging

Raj Purniman

***

The next morning was a replay of the day before, with Adi waking up rejuvenated, surrendering to his cup of morning tea under the hypnotizing trees. He carried forward his confidence in finding Nila and was hoping to meet Raj Purniman in the graveyard.

He was also contemplating other ways to find Nila if meeting Raj Purniman turned futile.

Adi's extended time with the morning tea made him skip his breakfast and shower once again, just in time to board the moving van. Once the van entered the graveyard, he saw a funeral crowd that had gathered already.

He had to join in the middle to assist the proceedings. He never resisted any of their requests, as he knew that the people were in pain. However, their pain was superseded by their hurry to finish the ceremonies on time.

Interestingly, after the first ceremony, there were no more visitors at the graveyard, which gave ample time for the volunteers to construct their grave. The participants were asked to do the ceremonies for life-sized dolls on which their name was written, symbolizing it was them.

Adi did the funeral ceremonies for his doll and was the sole spectator of the event.

The feeling of cremating himself had quite an effect on him in spite of his half-hearted participation. He felt liberated, once he was done with his cremation. He wondered about the meaninglessness of life and the futility of all the efforts humans took to run behind frivolous things.

Nearing dusk, a new wave of people entered the graveyard with their dead leader. Adi, who was exhausted, looked at the people who were crying for the dead man. They were drunk. Some were bursting crackers and dancing to the music.

He wondered, "What if there was nothing called life and death? And if they were irrelevant, why is there no peace in between?"

With the day getting busier towards the end, the only things that remained constant were the cries of anguish. The skies darkened and things settled down at the graveyard. Someone from the crowd handed Adi some whiskey that he gulped, sitting on his grave.

He tried to override memories of Nila with the intoxication and become unconscious. He was in no mood to slow down. The whiskey became water to his turbulent senses.

The intoxication was bringing out his worst fears and frustrations over his powerlessness to find Nila. He started walking around the graveyard, speaking to the dead ones beneath. Finally exhausted, he fell down in a drunken stupor, only to be carried back in the van. All the way back, the only word he kept mumbling between his lips was Nila.

***

The third morning, Adi did not hear the birds or the wind. He did not have his tea either and felt no peace. He was left with a terrible headache and an annoying hangover. He walked out and noticed that everyone had already left for their tasks. There was a flask placed outside his tent, with the covered breakfast.

Adi took his time to get over his condition. He had coffee, breakfast, and a hot shower. He was concerned about missing the trip to the graveyard when he thought about the possibility of meeting Raj Purniman. He started looking for someone who could help him to get there when he heard some noise behind the tents.

Adi walked there and noticed an old man in a white dress, trying to climb a tree to pluck gooseberries. Adi hid behind a tree and continued to watch the old man from a distance. After plucking the gooseberries, the old man jumped from the tree comfortably and started eating the fruit with an expressive smile. He was dancing with every bite.

He walked near the tree and placed his face on its bark with a smile. He then started collecting water from a tap and started filling the cups located at different locations. The old man's activities were so sharp and energetic that Adi continued watching him without getting bored. He noticed that birds flew near the old man fearlessly as if they knew him.

Adi walked towards him slowly. "Are you the caretaker of this place?"

The old man answered without bothering to turn back. "Not at all! This place is taking care of me."

Adi paused, unsure of how to react. The old man then turned to see Adi, smiling at him. He asked, "Have we met before?"

Adi didn't reciprocate his smile as the old man looked way too weird. He answered, "I don't think so!"

The old man smiled again. "It's fine, we are all related to each other, anyway."

Adi was reluctant to speak to the old man, who looked like he had lost his mind. However, with nobody around, he decided to give a try. With some hesitation, he asked, "Can I ask you a question?"

"Well, sometimes asking the right question is the answer by itself," the man replied with a grin.

The answer was a sharp blow to Adi's judgment. He felt that the old man must be some kind of a carefree saint. "Rightly said. But sometimes answers are needed as well! Are they not?"

The old man answered instantly, "The impulse to investigate can only be set free if you stop pretending to know answers that you don't."

Adi couldn't comprehend what he had just said. "I can see that you are a knowledgeable person. Are you a saint?"

"You judged me so soon!" The man laughed

"Oh God! What am I supposed to do? You aren't giving me answers!" Adi said, frustrated.

The old man smiled. "Exactly! When you have unanswered questions, you make God the answer."

"So, you don't believe in God," Adi observed, refusing to back down.

"It's an insignificant question. What difference is it going to make in our lives?"

Leaving Adi gaping at him, he moved to plant seeds at a shade.

"I guess you're an atheist. I am an atheist too… Just saying…" Adi tried to get in sync with the old man, who he felt was living in a different world.

"As an atheist, you have your faith, too!"

"So what's wrong in that? I believe that people worshipping their leaders are the same as the religious people worshipping their Gods!"

"Well, you try to justify your beliefs by proving someone else wrong. That is a false premise. It does not make your beliefs any stronger. Beliefs, if not allowed to change, become superstitions."

Adi found it hard to accept that he was unable to defend his views against an insane old man roaming in the hills. He felt that all his intelligence was falling flat on his face.

Thoughtfully, Adi asked, "I am just curious. Who taught you all this?"

The old man laughed, "Humans are nothing but their innate curiosity with their never-ceasing quest, this curiosity taught me all of this as well. The same curiosity that created science to explain the world will also bring the world to an end!"

Casually, the old man handed a bag of seeds to Adi and instructed him to plant them below the banyan tree near the temple.

Adi reluctantly received the seeds and started planting them, his mind still wavering around the old man and his wisdom. Once done with the planting, he mused, "You are forcing me to think a lot."

The old man said in a cautioning tone, "Please stop it. Thoughts cannot solve any problems. They are the problems themselves."

"Are you serious? You have an answer for everything, and yet every answer is a riddle in itself. What exactly do you want?" Adi asked, annoyed.

"Please guess that for me as well!"

"Salvation?"

"Salvation is also a form of desire. And with desire, life becomes a cascade where one goal leads to another."

"So you are telling me that you are perfect. You have no desire and no ego, isn't it?"

Realizing that Adi was getting angry without reason the old man smiled at him. "I am nobody to test your knowledge or ego. Nor have I ever proclaimed that I am perfect. But yes, life has taught me more than it has taught you because I have lived longer than you have. In spite of all the extra years I have lived, the right person from whom we can take a real opinion about life must be the newborn child who is yet to be polluted by this world."

Adi was calmed by the words. He stopped questioning and decided to listen to the old man, whose words were healing his soul.

After the talk, the old man asked Adi, "Are you here for the escape programme?"

"No, sir. I am here to meet Raj Purniman."

"Why?" asked the old man, with raised eyebrows.

"I want to speak to him about my wife, Nila."

With a curious look, the old man asked, "What happened to her?"

"Are you Raj Purniman?" asked Adi, seeing that the old man's face changed while mentioning Nila.

The old man nodded. "What happened?"

Adi was stunned. Collecting himself, he started narrating everything that happened, feeling peace at the end like he had gone through a counselling session.

The old man closed his eyes for a while and started speaking. "I met Nila a few times at the school for special children. I saw a lot of God in her. You are lucky to have married her. I remember, one time, she was speaking about adopting a baby from Syria. I don't know if she did that, but I remember the conviction in her eyes when she said this."

Raj Purniman suddenly opened his eyes, smiled at Adi and walked back to the trees playfully life before, totally unperturbed by the discussion he just had.

Adi felt all alone in the hills again, having more unanswered questions than he had before. He rushed back to his tent, collected his stuff and started walking down the hills in a hurry. He searched for his mobile phone and found it with its battery very low. He dialled a number.

"Qadir, don't speak anything now. I need your immediate favour."

"What?"

"Can you check if Nila or I had been to Syria recently?"

This time, the reply was the same, but in an entirely different tone. "What?"

✦✦✦

Dreams Come With Baggage

Adi opened the creaking doors of his office with renewed vigour, thanks to the four-day hiatus he had taken for trekking with Nila. His teams, deaf to the door's squeals, were glued to their systems totally unaware of his entry.

He took his seat, dusted his system and started checking his emails.

To his surprise, he found caustic reminders from two of their prominent client companies. Their latest emails were much beyond reminders. They were expressing their displeasure over the status of the respective projects.

One of them, Orez, had, in fact, terminated their contract, citing opportunistic loss owing to the project's delay. They absolutely refused to honour their payment commitments, even for the work that had been done thus far.

Adi felt numb and kept re-reading the mail for confirmation. He was not sure of his next move. His company was literally floating on the cash flow from these clients. Suddenly everything seemed to be sinking.

Adi paused. He wanted to consolidate the situation before talking to his team. Before he could decide, he received a call from Vaidya, Orez's General Manager.

"Why did you never pick our calls? What happened to your phone?" was the first question from Vaidya.

"I am extremely sorry sir. I was on a personal trip. And unfortunately, that place had no network. I came back only yesterday. Only after reading your emails did I get to know of the complications."

"That was an easy excuse, Adi. But I am afraid you need more than this to get us back as your clients!" Vaidya said stiffly.

"Sir, please give us just one more chance. We will get back on track in no time."

"Please don't start this now. You were given this project three months back. And till now, I don't see anything concrete. Trust me… Companies like ours don't run on hope but on results."

"Sir, I understand. But believe me, I am totally on this. I'll get all my resources to work on it. Please give me a breather."

"Not this time, Adi! I am the one on the receiving end for recommending your company. I have decided to stop connections with people who constantly make me sad. I am done with your company and team, but yes, you are always welcome as a freelancer like before."

Vaidya disconnected the call.

Adi was stunned again. The abrupt termination of the call, and with it, the client's association with his company, was too much to digest for him. He kept browsing through the mails. The only things he could see were reminders, discontented notifications, and complaints.

He looked at Ashish, who was busy coding next to him, and asked, "Did you check the emails?"

"Yeah… We tried contacting you but we couldn't reach you!" Ashish replied.

"Did you receive any phone from Orez or Wininfo?"

"Yeah. We informed them that you were out of town, and were expected only by next week."

"Great!" Adi muttered to himself.

He knew that being the youngest in his own company had its own shortcomings. 'What am I doing?' He asked himself.

He felt he was just killing time and money in this venture. Nothing substantial had materialized so far. He had to find a solution to keep his dream alive or perish under the burden of someone else's dreams.

***

Adi couldn't spend any more time at the office. He drove back home and remained in his car at the parking. He was annoyed, angry, feeling threatened by the course of events that had taken place at his office. He was clueless about what could turnaround the company's fortunes. He knew that he had no other choice. He considered calling Qadir, but decided against it, wanting to relax before discussing anything with others. He called Nila.

"Where are you?" he asked.

"I thought landlines don't move out of the house!" she replied.

"Okay, Madam Smart! What are you doing?"

"Well, I just came back after picking up Pari from school."

"Aren't you tired of ferrying her to and from school every day?"

"Not really, I love going there. By the way, how come you remembered me at this hour?" She asked curiously.

"I remember you all the time, Nila. Now just hop down to the parking spot. I am waiting."

Adi stretched himself, cracking his knuckles tiredly.

Nila didn't utter another word. She locked the door and rushed down.

She hugged Adi tightly. "Missed you so much already."

"Ready for a long drive?"

"Anytime!" She replied, excited.

The car zoomed out of the house into the loud city.

"Is something wrong?" she asked.

"Nothing," Adi replied focussing on the road.

"Just tell me... You'll be okay!"

"I am feeling better already Nila. Let's drive far today. I am sure the problems will disappear."

They drove through the city traffic amidst noises and pollution and got to the outskirts, which were relatively calmer and greener. Adi's mind, however, was stuck on the project he had lost, and the possible solutions for the problems at his office.

"Good or bad, I am me, and I think I have to make peace with it," Adi said out loud impulsively, ending the prolonged silence inside the car.

Nila did not reply, as she knew that Adi was talking to himself, and did not quite need her reply.

"So, what do you do at Pari's school?" Adi asked, wanting to break the silence on the long drive.

"Well, I have started volunteering there, and I help in training the kids as well."

"I hope you are enjoying it, and it's not due to some kind of obligation to Meera!"

"Not at all! I enjoy every bit of it. The school, the people, and mostly the kids. In fact, you must visit the school sometime. And if you are lucky, you can even meet Raj Purniman, its founder!"

"Mm... definitely!" Adi said, without much conviction. "But first let me finish the current commitments at work, and then I am all yours!"

"Fine then, finish it soon," she said, and added, "By the way, the last time I met Raj Purniman, he suggested that I should join their escape programme, and take you along as well!"

"Escape Programme? What's that? The name is interesting though!"

"I am not sure about it, but I heard that people from all across the country come to attend it."

"Well, as I said before, give me some time to get things back in place. After that, we are good to go," he replied with a wink.

After two hours, the car escaped the city outskirts and entered a village, with its scattered houses amidst crowded trees. Nila got a glimpse of a small pond on the way, which was still big enough to get her excited. She requested Adi to stop the car and suggested they halted for a while here.

Once out of the car, they realised that it was way cooler than the car's air conditioning inside. The chillness of the fresh breeze accompanied by the dark clouds hinted at imminent heavy rains, any moment which made the place exquisite.

"Can we go to the lake?" she asked.

"Now? Are you serious?" he replied, showing his lack of excitement with a relaxed shrug.

Nila requested again, trying hard this time, with a pleading face that Adi could never say no to. The couple started walking towards the pond and found the place more captivating than their expectations. The green space with flowers that grew all around brought Nila a lot of nostalgia. She was smiling all her way to the pond, like a little kid in a toy store.

"I just want to disappear into this," she said.

"What about me?" He asked, understanding her excitement.

She smiled. "I will take you with me as well."

The couple was exploring the place and its huge banyan tree when it started to drizzle. Adi ran to shelter himself whereas Nila walked towards the pond, getting fully drenched.

The feeling of soaking in the rain with the chill breeze and green trees all around was too overwhelming for her. She stepped into the pond and tears began to roll down her cheeks. She wished she could fly all over and spread this feeling onto everyone and everything.

"Are you alright?" he asked Nila, seeing her standing in the pond in the heavy downpour.

"Never better," she said, wiping her rainy tears.

Adi knew what exactly Nila was going through. His anxiety about the company and its future melted away with Nila's tears. He wished he could live like that.

Whatever his condition, Nila could make it beautiful just by being herself. Her unconditional love for life questioned Adi's priorities every time. He knew he could never become like Nila, who was full of life, but he also knew that he never wanted it in the first place. He felt complete just by being with her.

They spent some more time at the pond before heading back to the roads, when a heavy downpour made them quicken their footsteps. They rushed into the car and started watching the rain with the engines still off.

Nila noticed a cute little girl who was smiling at her from a distance and playing in the rain with her brother. The two kids laughed, giggled and even dived into a mud pool, enjoying every bit.

"Are we missing something?" Nila asked, holding Adi's hands.

***

Adi was restlessly waiting for the doctor's call, along with a dozen other couples who were awaiting their turn. He was the first one to arrive, but two other couples had been called in before him.

More than the anxiety for the test results, the need for the test itself was annoying him. He was willing to wait to have children, but Nila was way too eager to allow nature to take its own course.

"But why was I instructed to come alone?" he wondered. He was the only one without a pair.

"Mr. Aditya!" A nurse peeked out from the cabin, only to get back inside like the bird in a wall clock.

Adi went in immediately. The doctor, an old lady with thick glasses, was sorting through the results.

"Please be seated," she said, without even raising her head.

"Hope all is well, doctor!" Adi asked, sitting on the edge of the plastic chair.

The doctor did not reply, adjusting her glasses and reading the test report that Adi knew was his and Nila's. After rechecking the results, she looked up. "Mr. Aditya, I have gone through the test results thoroughly. Unfortunately, we found some issues. But there is no need to panic.

"What is it madam?" he asked, sliding to the tip of the chair.

"Well, your results are perfectly fine. But your wife's results suggest that she may have primary ovarian insufficiency. If this is confirmed, then I must say it's quite a rare thing to see in such a young age."

"Is that serious?" asked Adi, fearing the worst.

"This condition can be caused by a lot of reasons including family history, genes, etc., but given this state, she cannot become a mother unless she opts for alternate methods..."

Unable to come to terms with the fact that Nila had a medical issue, he held his pain within, and asked, "Will there be any problems to her health?"

"Not really. But remember, this condition may be for life, or it could become better on its own. Apart from fertility issues, she is perfectly fine. There could be frequent emotional swings, though. Hence your support is very important for her. Give yourself some time. You both are young, and you never know! Things might work out in your favour."

Adi took the results and thanked the doctor, still trying to make sense of the gravity of the discussion. The only solace he got out of the meeting was that Nila was safe. And this meant everything to him. He knew Nila would be shattered when she heard the news. As if his thoughts had reached her, he got a call from her.

"What did the doctor say?" she asked directly.

Adi paused, thinking of the posters he had seen during his wait. He invented wildly, "Well, there is nothing to worry! But she feels your haemoglobin levels are a bit low, and you should get a bit stronger before entering pregnancy."

"But what is delaying my pregnancy?" Nila was insistent, not allowing him to divert the question.

"Well, she says things are absolutely fine, but still we must delay pregnancy by a year so that we can expect a healthy kid!" He said in a single breath, trying hard to sound convincing.

There was complete silence on the other side, as Nila was unable to forego her dreams and come to terms with the doctor's suggestion. She asked in a low voice, "What do you think Adi?"

"Let's wait, Nila... Just one more year."

***

A lot was going through Adi's mind. He had a company to save, and a wife to care for. He wanted to take it slow, one thing at a time. He decided to get things back in shape at the company first. He reworked his strategies and started staying till late nights at the office, trying to keep up with the project's deadlines.

He also hired a few freelancers for assistance. This made him realise that a lot can be achieved by having a few committed, talented individuals instead of a crowd of mediocre people. Nila used to give him company once in a while. But Adi requested her to stay back at home, as he felt guilty of not spending enough time with her and letting her get bored with mundane office work.

Adi continued to be on his toes for days together, and yet he realised that keeping up with the deadlines was only next to achieving perfection as both were destined to be forever.

The only way he could live up to this was by adding more resources to the team. But he was sceptical about the change that the move could bring about.

Adi succeeded in completing one of the first major projects which he had committed to and was ready for its demo. It was only during his presentation that he came to know about the additional requirements the client had conveyed via mail, which had ended up going unnoticed.

Once the presentation was over, Adi was all alone at his office, contemplating the new requirement which altered the entire logic of the algorithm built so far, and was also questioning his own proficiency in running the company.

He knew that some decisions had to be taken before it was too late for him and the company. It was already dark outside when he noticed someone entering the office. On a closer look, he saw Nila standing at the door. He knew that something was wrong with her with the way she was approaching him.

Her face was pale, and she couldn't control her emotions when she saw Adi. She almost ran the last few metres and hugged him tightly, crying softly on his chest.

On instinct, Adi hugged her back. His heart pounded painfully. "What happened? How did you come here, all alone?"

"Pari left…" She said, her face still buried in his shoulders.

"What?" He asked again, fearing the worst.

"Pari and Meera left to America today," she replied, coming out of the hug this time and looking at his face.

He let out a big sigh. "You knew that before. They were supposed to go one day, anyway!"

Trying to compose herself, Nila said, "But I can't see them anymore. Even the mere thought hurts, Adi."

Holding Nila's face in his palms tenderly, he said, "People come and go all the time, Nila. You need to make peace with that. There are only a few constants in our life. Like me. I won't go anywhere! You know that!"

Looking sadly at Adi, she said, "First start coming home Adi. I feel distanced from you already."

"Well, in that case, I am calling it a day then. A long day, in fact."

He quickly collected his things and walked to the car. All the way home, he was consoling Nila.

The next morning, when Adi woke up and stretched, he saw Nila sitting quite close to him, holding a cup of coffee which was already half empty.

He grabbed the cup and sat up, looking curiously at her silent state.

"I want to adopt a child… From Syria," she said in a longing voice.

Adi almost spilled his coffee, looking at her in bewilderment.

"But why suddenly? And why Syria?" he managed to ask.

Nila pointed at the TV and increased the volume. The news channel showed images of children, some dead and many with blood all over them, being carried in varying stages of panic and emergency, by the volunteers in Syria.

The kids looked disoriented with shock and looked like they were more threatened by the chaos rather than their own little bleeding bodies.

***

"Wait, let me guess. You are closing down, right?" Qadir asked, pouring his second beer into the glass.

"Wow, I thought we would need a couple more rounds to arrive at that conclusion," replied Adi, who was still in his first.

"Well, lately, you have been giving many hints passively Adi. But listen, I own a company too, and I understand where you stand. I know that you can't change your core character to do business. But all I'd say is, try tweaking your business a little as per your traits. You gave life to it. You should give it your best before quitting."

"Like how, Qadir? My dream of making a successful company needs more than just me and my passion. But very clearly, I have decided to restrict my decisions to myself. And hence I've decided on giving up this dream."

"But why give up so soon? Take some more time. Your limit is not the world's limit. There are people out there somewhere, solving your problems already. All you need is to find that out!" Qadir said, frankly surprised by Adi's attitude.

"It's not a decision I made out of haste, Qadir. I've thought this through. The last few weeks have been exhausting. Especially monitoring people who don't share your vibe or resonate with your ideas."

"That will never actually happen, Adi. Expecting a person to listen to you and immediately get your vibe, is impossible. If you think you are in control, then automatically you are under pressure to get it right all the time."

Qadir paused, sipping his beer. "What about your team? How do they react to your orders?"

"Well, they all are hamsters on wheels. Too busy, but not productive. They look like they are working but the end product is never enough. They don't contradict anything I say, nor do they actively engage in discussions. And this makes my job even tougher."

Qadir remained quiet for a while, sipping his beer. "Just try to work out something, Adi. Nowadays, we have the opportunity to design our lives greater than ever."

"That's exactly my point, too. Why sacrifice your life for a company which anyway will be taken away by a big vulture if it succeeds?" Adi asked rhetorically.

"That's because the vulture will feed you in this deal. I know where you are arriving at, but do we have a choice? This will continue as long as we buy into their ideas, giving our lives in return."

"Whatever, Qadir! I intend to work as a freelancer again and continue to develop Apps. This way I think I will be at peace at least. I was definitely happier then. Had more time for myself and still made good money."

Qadir nodded mutely. He was already on his third beer, most of which he consumed in pensive silence.

"You know what, Adi? You are an old soul in a young body. You were different before... This new version of you is so far removed from who you were, who you are!"

Adi smiled sublimely. "What made you say that?"

"Well, interestingly... You are still on your first beer. And you are speaking of giving up. Need I say more?" Qadir shrugged.

"Priorities change, Qadir."

"Adi, I had a love marriage, too. But my life is just the same. Nothing changed drastically!"

"Please don't jump to any conclusions. Nila has nothing to with this decision of mine."

"Seriously?"

"Well, believe me... I am still sober when I am saying this. Nila is definitely a priority in my life. But more importantly, she made me understand the real priorities that I should have. I have this raw feeling of being me–just me–when I am with her. All other sophistications, including the fear of the future, the uncertainty, and doubts, disappear into thin air. And this means so much to me. She could have been a catalyst in my decision, but she's definitely not the sole reason."

Qadir remained silent, deep in thought. "Are you sure you are not drunk?" He asked with a dull smile. "By the way, there is one more reason why I came to meet you on a Sunday!"

Adi looked curiously, trying to guess, when Qadir interrupted, "I am shifting my company to America."

Adi knew that Qadir had been considering this move for a long time, as most of his clients were based out of that country. He just asked, "When?"

"Hopefully in a month's time… Things are getting sorted out really quickly," said Qadir, feeling slightly worried about leaving Adi behind. "Can you come with me, Adi?"

"Maybe later, Qadir. First, establish yourself there!" Adi replied, feeling emotional.

"Before I leave, I want you to do me a favour…" Qadir persisted.

"Tell me!" Adi demanded eagerly.

"For God's sake, finish your fucking beer!" Qadir snorted, letting loose a throaty laugh.

***

It was a Monday morning. Yet, Adi was in bed, stretching himself languidly. The bed coffee had been heated twice, but still couldn't convince him to open his eyes. Nila was worried. She touched Adi's forehead, but couldn't make much out of it. He looked and felt normal.

She lay beside him for a while, but once she realised that he was more comfortable with the pillow than with her, she decided to leave him alone.

After hours of extended sleep, Adi opened his eyes and muttered to himself. "I am going to be free again. This is how a Monday morning should be!"

He heated his coffee for the third time and looked out for Nila, who was glued to the news channel.

"Nila... Don't tell me it's Syria again?!" he exclaimed, wanting to discuss his company closure plans, as well as his next course of action.

"Not just Syria... Everything looks so sad." Nila replied, with her eyes still glued to the TV screen.

"Learn to ignore it, Nila. It's a big world out there, and only bad things get projected for TRPs." Adi said, sipping his coffee.

"But whenever I see all of this, I feel responsible... And I am sad that I couldn't do anything about it."

"That's ridiculous! Stop taking things personally. You are not even sure what is true and what is not. News media today is nothing but corporate houses running after profits. So please stop bothering about it."

"But... What if it's true Adi? Can't we do something about it?"

"We will do our part. But again, there are plenty of others who are working day in day out to make this world a better place. You know the stories, don't you?"

Nila remained quiet for a while and then nodded. "Why didn't you go to your office today?"

Adi smiled. "Well, that is something I was planning to talk to you about before all these discussions cropped up!"

"Are you closing the company?" Nila asked instantly.

Adi was stunned, wondering how easy it sounded in her voice.

"Yeah, something like that... But it's just a pause button!"

He then explained his plans of becoming a freelancer, detailing how his work routines could change, and what they should be prepared for. While talking, he noticed that Nila's eyes were on him, but her thoughts were elsewhere.

"What are you thinking?" he asked, stopping abruptly.

"Nothing," she replied, shaking herself.

"It's fine, Nila. You can tell me what you feel about my decisions. I am starting something new, and your ideas are integral to my plans as well..."

"Well I wanted to do a few things, and I am not sure if you will be ok with them!"

He looked at her inquisitively. "What are they?"

"I want to visit my village once."

"Done! Even I wanted to visit the village, and my old friend Lal," Adi smiled. "What's next?"

"I want both of us to enrol in the escape programme of Raj Purniman."

Adi scratched his chin thoughtfully. "How long is the programme?"

"I don't know... They say it depends on the individual taking the programme!"

"Well, I can't promise you that until I know the details... But yes, if it can fit into our schedule, then why not?"

Nila didn't look happy with Adi's partial approval. She looked down before voicing her third request. "There is one more thing left, Adi!"

"I am all ears." He said earnestly.

"I want to adopt a child from Syria," she said, with her eyes fixed on the floor.

Adi grew pale. He walked out of the room, to get seated in the swing. Only he knew Nila's medical condition. And yet, it wasn't enough to convince him to adopt a child, especially from a place like Syria. He contemplated it for a while. He walked back into his room and realised that she was still sitting in the same place.

"Nila, you don't understand the seriousness of Syria. Why don't we adopt a kid somewhere else?

With tears in her eyes, Nila replied, "You know that I was saved from a forest fire which took away my entire family!"

Hearing the pain in her voice, Adi felt torn. He sat down beside her and held her hands gently. "I know that. But please don't relate that with this, Nila. We can still adopt someone in need, and it will still make a difference."

"When I saw those kids running in Syria, I felt there was some child out there, waiting for us…" Nila choked on her tears and hugged Adi desperately.

Adi was tormented by conflicting emotions. He held Nila in his arms, comforting her, trying to understand her perspective. Good or bad, he had to take a decision that would impact both him and Nila hugely. He looked at the television, with its loud news coverage of the Syrian war. The footage was gory but something else caught his attention. There was a news scroll at the bottom, calling for donations and volunteers.

He kissed Nila on her head and said, "We will go to your village first, and then we shall decide our next move." Looking at the people crowding for food in a Syrian war camp in the television, Adi thought, 'So these people won't be strangers anymore!'

✦✦✦

Journeys Can Be Destinations

Adi heard a knock that interrupted his sleep. He woke up in a hurry, feeling woozy, and fell onto the floor without control. He got back on his foot, undeterred by the ankle sprain, and limped out to the doors, expecting a miracle. But it was Qadir who was waiting at the doors, with a set of papers.

Looking at Qadir, Adi's excitement vanished in an instant, leaving him pale. However, he tried to hide his disappointment and welcomed Qadir, who did not miss the obvious disinterest. Wordlessly, Qadir entered the house, helped himself to a glass of water, and walked out to the balcony, escaping the feeling of suffocation inside. Adi followed him and took his place on the swing. Qadir remained standing, with his glass.

"Got any Information?" Adi asked.

Qadir didn't say a word, trying hard to control himself. He asked patiently, "When was the last time you saw yourself in a mirror?"

"That's not the priority at the moment, Qadir. Just tell me, did you get any information?"

"Not a priority? Are you kidding me? Look at you, Adi! You have become a skeleton. Have you stopped eating altogether?" Qadir asked, his volume rising with every word.

Adi did not answer. He was impatient but understood that Qadir was upset too. So he remained quiet to allow Qadir to relax a bit.

"You know what, Adi? I am equally guilty in this. If I had not gone to America, none of this would have happened. In fact, I am happy that I came back at least now. Or I don't know if I would have ever seen you again!" Qadir said. "Last I remember, you sent me a single message, saying that you were going to Nila's village, and would be unreachable for a while. That's all you had to say to me."

"No matter how many times you ask me this, I have no answer, Qadir. How do you expect me to answer you when I am clueless myself?" Adi exclaimed, unable to remain silent anymore.

"Whatever... If you were really interested in being in touch with me, you would have found a way. But you didn't, and that's the end of the discussion," Qadir shot back, letting out his frustration.

"I don't know what to answer, Qadir. I just don't know!"

They both remained quiet for a while, with the silence filling Adi with guilt and Qadir with disappointment. Qadir, however, tried to get back his composure. He no longer wanted to disturb Adi, who was already in deep distress.

"Is there anything at all you could remember? I mean I am finding it difficult to accept any of this... You must be getting at least some parts of your memory back!"

"Do you remember your second day at school, Qadir?" asked Adi in return.

"What? Are you serious?" Qadir asked, feeling annoyed by the question.

"Well, that's exactly what is going through my head. And the agony is, I don't know what part of my memories I had naturally lost to time, and what else due to the accident."

Qadir felt his anger ebbing away. He looked at Adi. "You never cease to puzzle me, man, with or without your memory!"

Adi replied with a smile. "So, did you get the information I asked for?"

"Yes, and that will be the biggest puzzle you will ever hear in your life," Qadir replied.

"What?"

"You have been to Syria with Nila..."

Adi didn't reply. A million thoughts ran through his mind.

"You have been to Syria with Nila, and you both were enrolled as volunteers under Red Cross." Qadir continued calmly, trying to understand Adi's reaction.

Adi remained silent. He couldn't believe that so much had happened, and yet he was completely clueless. "Did you contact the Red Cross?" he asked.

Qadir nodded, "Yes, but they have no further information about Nila after she reached Syria. In fact, there was no information about you either until I told them about you."

"Can Nila be somewhere in a hospital like me?" Adi asked.

"Don't you remember? Contacting hospitals was the first thing we did. And even the police are trying to trace her everywhere. But to me, the more important question is, why Syria? Why did you go to a country in war, and that too as a volunteer?"

Adi's eyes were fixed on the ground. "I don't know about the volunteer part. But I do remember Nila wanting to adopt a child from Syria."

"Mm..." Qadir said thoughtfully. "Well, that explains the volunteer part as well. Since it's the only way you can enter the country. But then again, don't you think going to Syria for adopting a baby is a tad too much? Even considering the humanitarian angle…"

"Please, Qadir. Don't go there again. After all of this, I believe anything is possible. Something must have happened, so I am not surprised if it's outrageous. In fact the more absurd it seems, the easier it becomes to explain the mess I find myself in." Adi said, trying to pacify Qadir as well as himself.

"I don't think I can ever figure out your life, Adi. It has been always outrageous… In some way or the other. And I don't think if I can handle these many adversities, like the ones life has been throwing at you. All I know is that I want to help you, no matter what."

"Even I am tired. Nila is all that I want in my life now, and I am done with my aspirations and adventures," Adi said, letting out a deep breath.

Qadir looked at Adi, and sadness engulfed him. He tried to divert himself.

"Okay, now let's get back to work. You were in Syria as a volunteer. But how did you intend to adopt a baby in a Muslim country that is in war? Their laws are too stringent for adoption, I guess…"

Adi shrugged, unable to offer anything constructive.

Deciding to browse the internet to learn more, both Adi and Qadir sat with their laptops on the swing. Qadir was correct in assuming that adoption was almost impossible in Syria. That was the reason Syrian orphans were adopted through authenticated agencies, predominantly present in Turkey.

This was also done to minimize the possibility of human trafficking, helping good-intentioned people with getting an authenticated orphan child to adopt.

“So are you going to Turkey now?” asked Qadir.

“First of all, you have to understand that I am on the same page as you. I am just making all possible assumptions to decide my next move.”

“Well, in that case, think some more to come up with something concrete… Until then I’ll make some coffee for us,” Qadir said, and walked into the kitchen.

Adi remained in the swing, unable to even coherently imagine the events that had happened in his life. The thought of Nila being stuck alone in Syria was horrifying.

He started contemplating all the possibilities to get her back, including support from the government as well as using social media. He was lost in thoughts when Qadir returned with some black coffee for both.

“So, decided anything?” Qadir asked, giving Adi his cup.

“Qadir, I went to Syria once already for Nila. And I will go again for her. I need your help this time…”

“What? Do you even understand what you are asking?”

“I know, Qadir. But trust me, this is my last chance of finding Nila. I just can’t just sit here and hope that someone will find Nila for me. I can’t take any chances anymore.”

“Now, don’t rush to conclusions. A lot of damage has been done already. Take your time, think this through, and tell me.”

Adi didn’t reply, as he pondered. Qadir, meanwhile, was looking at Adi, deep in thought. His reddened eyes, with dark circles around them, the unshaven beard and lean stature were way too much to digest for Qadir. His eyes got moist.

He couldn’t bear the sorrow Adi was going through. He cursed himself for not being there for Adi when needed and decided to get him to Syria no matter what.

"There is one condition, Adi, if you need to go to Syria." Qadir offered softly.

"What?" Adi asked, surprised by Qadir's sudden words.

"I will come with you."

Adi felt both exhausted and frustrated. "Please, don't do this Qadir. Don't get emotional over this. I am going there with the belief that you will take care of the search operations here. She can be anywhere, Qadir, and you double my strength by being here. Please understand me."

Qadir nodded and left the place, unable to look at Adi's sorrowful eyes. "I'll be back soon, Adi."

Qadir had underestimated the struggle involved in getting the job done. It occurred to him that becoming a volunteer and getting associated with an NGO was the way forward for Adi, as his travel might need a lot of movement within the country in order to search Nila. Qadir had to choose the area of volunteering according to Adi's skill, as well as his requirements in Syria. He had never expected becoming a volunteer to serve the needy could be this hard.

He understood that, no matter what, the world was never in a hurry to listen to one's demands, it's all left to every individual to live up to its standards.

It was more than a fortnight later when Adi received a message from Qadir, asking to meet him immediately at his office. But Adi decided to call him first.

"What is it Qadir?" he asked anxiously.

"Your papers are ready, Adi. You are now a legal volunteer to serve the land of Syria again."

There was no reply but Qadir could hear Adi's heavy excited breathing.

Qadir said again "Adi, I know what you are capable of. But please remember to be safe, once you are in Syria, it won't be just Nila who will be waiting for you. But yes, get her back, man. We all need a happy ending, and I need my old Adi back."

***

Adi was at Syria, standing outside the Aleppo International airport, waiting for his cab, when he noticed an ambulance rushing to the Airport. He realised that the injured victims were the volunteers who had been serving in the war.

He ran after the ambulance to know more.

But he heard a voice from behind. "Never look there unless you are planning to go that way."

It was the driver of the cab who had come to pick Adi up. Adi turned back to look at the driver, who looked more like a philosophy teacher, with his beard and the glasses, than a cab driver.

"Are you Aditya?" The driver asked.

"Yeah," Adi replied and wondered how his simple name could sound so different.

"I just can't understand what makes people visit Syria. Is it some kind of an adrenaline rush or something which adds to one's Resume?" the driver asked, helping Adi with his baggage.

Adi did not answer the question, although he knew that the driver was trying to understand his reason for visiting Syria.

When the car started, Adi noticed a gun protruding from the driver's pant. The driver noticed Adi looking at it, and pushed the gun deeper into his pockets, concealing it with his shirt.

"It's just for my safety, and I don't intend to use it, although I have been carrying it with me forever. Even if I had to use it, I know it will be my last time," said the driver.

Adi couldn't understand the gravity of the driver's statement. He was already disillusioned by the new territory, with its new people.

He was anticipating a worrying situation in the country, but the views he got of the city during his journey presented a different picture. After an hour's drive through the nearly empty roads, they reached his hotel. He was handed over the keys and was informed that he had to share his room with another volunteer who had already arrived.

Every step he took in this country made him wonder if Nila had been there at those places. He had pasted Nila's picture at the back of his shoulder bag, just on the off chance that someone would recognize her, and speak to him about her.

Adi entered the room and noticed someone sleeping in the bed, fully covered. He placed his luggage and approached the window to look at the view outside. The place looked relatively calm for a nation in war.

Adi's mind was clouded by the tasks he must complete, and the places he must visit to search for Nila.

This had made him blind to the seriousness of the situation in Syria, which he might have otherwise noticed from the very second he boarded the flight. Adi saw a coffee maker in the room and made a hot cup for himself. He settled down in a wooden chair placed at the little balcony, surprised at the different taste of the drink.

"Are you from India?" asked a voice from behind him.

A dark, lean, man was pushing a chair for himself inside the balcony. He made himself comfortable near Adi.

Adi nodded.

"That's nice. I am Thiru from Germany," the man introduced himself.

"I am Aditya. I can't help but observe that except for your slang, you look like an Indian, too."

"Well, the only way I am related to India is that it is close to my country, Ceylon – I mean Sri Lanka. I had lived there until I had to uproot myself to run for my life."

Reflecting on Thiru's statement, Adi replied, "Well, I knew a little about the war that happened there, but never knew people got settled in such faraway places... I had always presumed India is a safer haven, and closer to your country as well, making it easier to settle there."

"It's nice of you to accept the fact that you know only very little about the war. It's better that way, or else I would have talked a lot and messed a rare serene morning in a noisy country like this."

Adi was taken aback on hearing such an outright statement from a person who was still a stranger to him. He said, "I am sorry if I had disturbed you in any way..."

"Not at all. I wish I can erase my past memories, but unfortunately, it's only those memories which have made me what I am today. My people ran to different countries for asylum during the war. However, people like me, who ran far, are doing great. But the ones who ran to their neighbouring countries like India are still living like refugees, shunned into solitude by hatred!"

Adi felt bad for starting this discussion and obviously upsetting Thiru. "I am really sorry to hear all this. I had always assumed otherwise. And whatever I know comes from the news media. I have no clue about it."

Thiru smiled. "Sorry if I was rude. That's my way of talking!"

Adi waved the apologies aside and stood up to get ready for the day.

"Never seen an independent volunteer from India so far... You must be different." Thiru observed, as Adi was about to move.

"It's too early for you to judge me," Adi replied nonchalantly. "Anyway... What makes you a volunteer here?"

"Memories. My memories make me do this. I am trying to make up for the lost opportunities in the past," Thiru replied.

"It's really nice knowing you, Thiru. I didn't come here for volunteering work. I am here in search of my wife"

"What? But how did you lose her?" Thiru asked, surprised.

"It's a big story to start the day with. Her name is Nila. Rings any bells?"

"No, but I can try to help you with my sources here. I have been here longer and know some people who can put you in the right direction. Did your wife come here to volunteer too?"

"Yes. That will be great, thank you. By the way, what's the status of the war? How easy is it for me to move around?"

"Well, wars are business deals and will end when the deal is struck. Until then, people are kept busy running for their lives."

***

Adi walked down the vintage stairs to report at the reception, where he saw a bunch of youngsters awaiting their coordinator. They were herded to a hall for a quick orientation and were briefed about the massive bomb blast that had happened in Aleppo city the previous day, causing severe casualties, and unmanageable crowds at the hospitals.

The volunteers were supposed to support the physicians at the hospitals that day, as they were all trained in First Aid.

The youngsters were excited to be in action, as this was a new experience for most of them in the group. Adi, however, was still confused about his next course of action. Being from a totally different background, and in the country for a different purpose, he felt too alien.

This was apparent from the way the others were looking at him. The rush of the youngsters and their energy was too radiant for Adi. But he joined the team, and landed at the hospital amidst all the chaos.

Adi was allotted a line of beds, where he was supposed to stay and monitor the patients throughout the day. There were hardly any doctors, and only the volunteers were attending to the patients. Since it was a secondary hospital, it was essentially utilized to hold the patients with minor injuries.

The serious cases were transported to the General Hospital in the Capital City. Adi continued assisting the patients, feeling restless within for not doing enough to start with his search for Nila.

Most of the patients in the line allotted to Adi were old people, who were admitted after being suffocated in the smoke and fire from the bomb blasts.

They were under ventilation support, and Adi had to check the parameters of the equipment and other vitals of the patient at frequent intervals. As Adi was marking the levels on one of the instruments, he saw Thiru coming from the next room.

"What are you doing here?" Thiru asked.

Adi felt a huge sigh of relief, seeing a familiar face in that alien land. “I don’t know what I am supposed to do. It’s all happening so fast that I could hardly find time to speak to anybody.”

Thiru nodded, “It’s not that you are not being helpful here. But no one can help you but yourself. It’s your life and no one can walk in your shoes.”

“Frankly, I don’t know where to start, Thiru!” Adi confessed. He was sweating profusely in the hot and humid environment. There was a power outage with no backup power even.

“Well, meet the volunteering team coordinator… Perhaps he might be able to help you.”

“Okay, but I’m finding it difficult to communicate with the people here,” Adi said, wiping sweat from his forehead.

“Are you serious? For God’s sake, they are volunteers too! Go speak to them…” Thiru replied, a bit louder this time.

He took over the responsibility from Adi and asked him to find the coordinator. As Adi started enquiring with the hospital authorities, he came to know that the coordinator had left the place to take two critical accident victims to the main hospital. They were also not sure about the time of his return. On Adi’s insistence, he was directed to an ambulance which was ready for its third trip to the main hospital, carrying more victims.

As Adi hopped on, the ambulance driver smiled at him, much to his surprise. Adi reciprocated back a bit hesitantly. The ambulance was carrying a mother and a kid who were gravely injured by shelling over Aleppo. The injured kid's twin brother was seated beside Adi, and was in a state of shock, unable to comprehend what was happening in front of him.

"Why do they still live here amidst all this? They should move to the Zaatari camp until things are under control," said one of the volunteers.

"It's not that easy for them, Madam," said the driver. "They believe they have a legacy here, although it is reduced to rubbles now. Every morning, they come out, believing things were going back to normal, and run back to their hiding spots at dusk just to make sure they live through the night."

"Whatever it is, they have no rights to impose this suffering on their children. These kids have seen nothing but war all through their life, and we are yet to analyse the psychological impact it will have on them," said the volunteer.

Listening to this, the nurse in the ambulance said, "Finally someone said it. We are all busy treating the physical bruises and wounds but then… we are getting the bodies of many teenagers who have committed suicides. Unfortunately, these suicide cases are more in the refugee camps which we consider as the safest haven."

The volunteer's eyes got moist listening to it.

Holding her emotions in check, she said, "How cruel could the world be? There are countries where people with no job are pampered with money and food, whereas here even the new-born infants should make peace with the war. I don't understand who gives these assholes the authority to dictate others' lives. I am sick and tired of the shelling sounds, and the smell of blood everywhere. If this is how life has to continue, then I wish this everything would come to an end by some mega bomb that will wipe out everything instead of leaving the country and its people broken... I am ready to die with everybody"

The ambulance was stained with more tears than blood this time. Adi, though silent, felt guilty and sad. His primary worry was finding his wife, but it did not make him less immune to these human emotions.

The bleeding body of the kid with his unconscious mother beside him was heart-wrenching. He tried hard to control his emotions until the kid in shock hugged him, and cried for his mother. The ambulance reached the hospital, and the patients were rushed to the Emergency Ward while the volunteer decided to retain the kid with herself, in order to keep him safe from the traffickers.

The ambulance driver, after assisting in shifting the passengers, approached Adi eagerly and gave him a firm handshake.

"You know him before?" the other volunteer asked the driver.

"Madam, I have seen many volunteers in my life who come to serve this country valiantly. But I've never seen any volunteer getting injured in this war, and still coming back to serve. He is the first one!" The driver said, pointing at Adi with a small salute.

***

Adi was seated at the Aleppo University Hospital's canteen with the ambulance driver and was excited by the fact that someone had identified him in Syria

"I am Adi, and you are?" Adi started slowly, trying not to allow his curiosity to take over.

"I am Salim," the driver replied.

"Salim, I am really glad that you recognized me. But quite frankly, I don't remember a thing that happened to me here. The injury which you were referring to, has taken away all my memory associated with this place," Adi tried to explain everything at a go.

Salim couldn't comprehend what Adi was trying to say. It seemed incomprehensible for a person who looked and behaved normally but insisted that he was not. Finally, Salim managed to say, "I don't understand, sir."

Adi looked at Salim's puzzled face and decided to go slower this time. He spoke in detail about his accident, about Nila, and also about their adoption plans which had brought them to Syria. He told everything he knew and explained that he had forgotten the rest.

Salim kept listening to Adi intently and was amused as he had never heard anything of this kind before.

"But why did you come again, sir? You could have taken the help of your country's embassy!" Salim asked.

"Those methods take time, and they cannot even find a person if they have all the information, which I can clearly not provide. Even the local police in my country are unable to trace because I could not tell them much. But every day delayed pushes me farther from Nila. Well, I can't wait anymore. I have to find her myself."

Salim understood Adi's desperation. He said consolingly, "Sir, all I could remember about that night was that you were injured by the shelling, and volunteers were all around you, trying hard to save you!"

"Did you see any woman with me while I was wounded?" Adi asked.

Salim shook his head sadly.

"Was there any Indian lady in a volunteer uniform that day?"

"There were many ladies volunteering, and I am not sure about their nationality, sir."

"What should I do now?" Adi asked, unable to decide on his next move.

"Let's meet the doctors at the Emergency Ward sir. They might recognize you..."

"Do you think they can? Especially after all this while?" Adi asked, disappointed with the lack of leads.

"I recognized you, sir, didn't I?"

Salim walked towards the Emergency Ward amidst all the cries, while Adi followed him, matching his every step. Salim was immune to the blood stains on the floor and didn't react to the people calling out to him for help, as he knew he couldn't be of much help there when doctors themselves were helpless.

Adi, however, was feeling guilty for rushing through, and not bothering to listen to their pleas.

Looking straight ahead and walking briskly, Salim said, "Sir, nothing here is your fault. Unfortunately, it is the good people who feel sad even if the mistakes are made by the bad ones."

These words didn't convince Adi, who felt this was not the way one should look at life. As Salim reached the Emergency Ward, he asked Adi to wait at the hall and entered the doctor's cabin.

Adi felt terrible there, seeing that many patients there were literally bleeding to death. Operations were being performed in the General Ward with limited equipment and drugs.

The limited number of beds in the hospital couldn't stop the entry of new emergency cases along with their loved ones, adding chaos and distress.

The beds were allotted based on the gravity of the injury, or the stubborn insistence of the attendees.

The people who were not really badly wounded were left to fight for the stain-free floor spaces.

"Are you alright?" Salim asked gently.

"Yeah, I am fine," Adi replied, wiping his tears in a hurry.

"I think we have found the right person to talk to you," Salim informed, slightly excited.

"Who is that?"

"The doctor who treated you," Salim replied, taking Adi to a small cabin.

The doctor was an old lady, who was speaking to a young mother about her son.

The mother was visibly furious with the doctor, and she stalked out of the room shouting loudly all the way. But the doctor remained calm as she injected some pain killers into the kid's body.

Adi was shocked to see the kid, with one of his legs amputated. He felt uncomfortable and restless to stand beside the injured kid.

"Is he still bleeding?" he asked, looking at the unconscious kid.

"Well, the blood loss is contained as of now, but I am afraid that we cannot arrange for any more blood if he needs it in the future. There is a dearth of blood supply, as our biggest blood unit was destroyed during the last airstrike."

"Will he be alright, doctor?" Adi asked again.

"Don't worry. He will be alright. By the way, I am Dr. Dyab, and I gave you First Aid when you were injured," said the doctor.

Adi felt bad as he could not identify the doctor who had treated him. He was guilty about disturbing her in the middle of her job.

Since the doctor had started the conversation about his injury, he hesitated only a second before asking, "Anything else you remember about that night, madam?"

"Well, Salim informed me about your problem. I have no clue about your wife, but I remember a nurse speaking about you and your wife the other day. She is off duty right now, but we have called her in since the patient count is very high today. You can wait here for her… The situation outside is bad." The doctor said apologetically.

Salim, who was sitting beside Adi, asked Dr. Dyab, "Madam, why was the lady shouting at you before?"

"Oh, she is this child's mother. She is too upset to see her son this way, and wanted to kill him and end all his pain once for all," Dr. Dyab said in a soft tone, washing her hands.

"How can she say that?" Adi asked, stunned. "The kid can still live to see the world. What more does a mother want?"

Dr. Dyab paused, looked at the kid, and replied "It is not death that these people fear, but the loss of their abilities to survive the war. This kid has become vulnerable and more prone to suffer in the war just because he has lost his leg, and a huge extent of his mobility"

"But this war will come to an end, won't it?" Adi asked, refusing to accept the statement.

"That is something we are hoping for every day. But days have turned into weeks, months and years… And yet all we fear is, which direction the next attack will be from!"

Dr. Dyab wiped her face with the towel and sat down on her chair. Looking at the kid, she said, "You know what? I have been in practice for the last 30 years, and I was on the verge of retirement when this war started. I have never seen anything like this in my whole life, not even in my textbooks.

I was a gynaecologist, but now I am forced to do all kinds of operations due to the shortage of doctors."

She paused and continued. "I must say that it's not only the wounded and dead people who should be counted as victims of war crimes but also people like us – doctors, nurses, and volunteers who continue to spend their days and nights amidst these cries and sorrow. "

"Our lives have been stolen by this war, just like every other person living and dying in this country." She insisted.

Hearing the rare outburst, Salim went to Dr. Dyab, trying to console her. Adi sat unmoving, cursing the war and his fate in having to witness all this sadness.

Just as Dr. Dyab and Salim were conversing in low voices, an old woman with a bandage on her head approached them for medicine to cure her pain.

Dr. Dyab opened a drawer, took out a tablet strip, and handed it over. "Have one in the morning and one in the night. Sometimes the pain will be there. But that indicates that your wound is healing fast."

The lady thanked Dr. Dyab and kissed her hands before leaving the room.

"Are you sure they were the right medicines?" Salim asked curiously.

"Why did you ask that?" Dr. Dyab asked, surprised.

"Well, the drawer had only that medicine, and nothing else"

Dr. Dyab smiled. "You are right about the medicine... But don't worry, it's just a placebo. We're running short of basic medicines, so we are forced to ration drugs till we get new supplies. Unfortunately, ever since we had started getting the medicines and supplies through international aid, the local pharmaceutical industry has started to disappear. Now, even in an emergency, we have to wait for the aid as there is no local supply anymore."

Salim acknowledged Dr. Dyab's statement and added, "That's the fate of Syria today. They are now used to getting everything free… So all productive businesses have slowed down, leaving everyone lazy."

Dr. Dyab turned to Adi, who looked disturbed. "Our country was never like this. You should have come to this place a decade ago, and you would have been impressed. Those were days when terminally ill patients preferred to take their chances to extend their life even by a couple of months. But today, even the little ones can't take the agony of living one more day in this hell." she said.

Adi nodded desolately, "I relate to every single word of yours. I know you are tired, and in fact, I feel guilty to be disturbing you in the middle of all this. But I promise to do everything I can, once I find my wife."

Dr. Dyab smiled at Adi. "Don't worry, Allah will be with you."

She could not sit up for long as she was exhausted from continuous work. She excused herself and lay down on the floor. Adi and Salim got up to leave, seeing that she was trying to catch up some sleep while she could. But just as Dr. Dyab started taking deep breaths, there was loud shouting in the ward.

An attender rushed to Dr. Dyab's room and shouted at her for sleeping when her husband was going into shock. Dr. Dyab woke up in an instant and was trying hard to get up from the floor, assisted by Adi and Salim. She took her stethoscope and rushed outside.

Salim followed her, just in case she needed someone for help.

Adi remained in the room and didn't want to be in the middle of any scene. He bent over the table, thinking about all that was happening around him. His exhausted body tricked his mind to confusion and slowly he fell into a fitful sleep when he started hearing loud noises again.

He opened his eyes to see Dr. Dyab and Salim entering the room. He was awake in an instant.

"He was bound to die anyway… Why couldn't they accept it?" asked Salim, saddened by the deep woes of the dead man's wife and mother at the ward.

"Everyone knows that death will happen to all of us eventually. And yet we are infinitely shocked when it happens to someone we love. They would have expected one more chance, but when that is denied, they are shaken. After all these deaths, I have learned more about life than about medicines."

As they were talking, a young nurse with drowsy eyes entered the room and greeted Dr. Dyab. She looked at Adi and her drowsiness vanished in an instant. She smiled graciously at him.

"I have heard a lot about you, sir," she said.

Adi looked surprised by her statement. Dr. Dyab interrupted, "This is the nurse I was talking to you about. She is Munira."

Munira smiled again at Adi and said, "I have seen you once before when you visited this hospital with your wife for volunteering. Although I couldn't talk to you, Nila befriended me quickly. She discussed her adoption plans and even told me how much both of you loved kids…"

Adi's eyes grew moist when heard Munira taking Nila's name. He asked her, "Do you know where she is?"

“I don’t know exactly, but I remember a friend of mine telling me that he had seen Nila in one of the relief camps in Madaya.”

There was a moment of silence in the hall.

“Anything else you know which can guide us?” Salim asked.

“Nothing much… Even the conversations I had with Nila were not about anything specific, although she spoke to me as if she had known me for years.”

Adi couldn’t stop the tears rolling down his face. He composed himself. “What else did she speak about? Please don’t mistake me… I just can’t stop myself from wanting to hear more about her. Thoughts of her are my only solace now!”

Munira felt sorry for Adi. She sat near him and described everything she remembered, based on her discussion with Nila, starting from her dresses to her interests in knowing about the kind of plants that grow in Syria.

The talk continued for a while, rejuvenating Adi enough to begin the next leg of his journey towards Madaya, in search of Nila despite being warned about that place at present. He thanked Dr. Dyab and Munira for their support and concern.

Just as Adi was about to leave, Dr. Dyab held his hands and said, “I wish you all the luck. And do remember to keep your heart strong for us. This world is unconditional for both love and hate. It needs more people like you.”

Salim got up too, got blessings from Dr. Dyab and said to Adi, “Sir, let’s go to Madaya.”

***

The trip to Madaya started relatively normally, except for the unusual engine noise of the ambulance. The roads were deserted, and so was the city. Adi felt that every inch of the soil was tainted by acts of violence. There was bloodshed everywhere, even on long forgotten buildings and roads.

"Where have they all gone?" Adi asked.

"Most people have fled this place, and are living as refugees in some neighbouring countries, especially Jordan. The Zaatari camp in Jordan holds the maximum Syrian refugees."

"How is their life there?" Adi asked, remembering Thiru's words.

"Sir, no other country can be equal to one's motherland. Also, these people are refugees. No one treats them with respect. They are shown only pity. But refugees are not in a mind to see all this. They are just protecting themselves and their loved ones, even at the cost of selling their souls."

"What about you, Salim? Where is your family?"

Salim paused and composed himself at this unexpected question. "I lost my parents long ago. I was an engineer but the war made me a driver. It also got my only brother stuck in jail."

Adi was saddened. "Why?"

"I wish I knew the answer, sir. Crime here is defined by the Government, based on its whims and fancies. Nothing is permanent."

"Well, then why don't people hide from all this until things sort out?"

"Easier said than done, sir. Anyway let me tell you what happened with my brother, so you can get a hang of things happening here."

Salim started with his story, as he knew that they had a long distance to cover before arriving at Madaya.

"This happened during the revolts, when the army was harsh on the civilians, especially the youngsters. A friend of his was dropping my brother at his college when he was interrupted by the soldiers, who got him arrested for driving without a license. My brother was terribly upset with this, and he wanted to get his friend out somehow. But no legal means worked, and no one told him where his friend was jailed. He tried for months with no response.

"Eventually, he tried to rob a store to bribe the authorities and get his friend released. He ended up being arrested in this process. It's been almost a year now, and I am yet to see him. He could have just spoken to me before doing any of this foolishness…" Salim said, feeling emotional after thinking of his brother.

Adi remained silent, allowing Salim to compose himself.

But Salim continued. "This is how a small event gets blown up, sir. Now when youngsters like him come out of jail, they will be devoid of any social status. Even the government denies them their basic privileges. They become vulnerable and are easy prey to the terror outfits that pull him in under the disguise of a rebel. They seem to give these misguided youngsters the validation they crave. And in turn, these blinded people vent out their anger. Eventually, it becomes too late for them to regret. I have been seeing this misery repeating continuously, and yet nothing could be done. This is agony, sir…"

"It's terrifying. There has to be some way to deal with this. Or else, with the way things are going, nothing will remain."

"What can I say, sir? Syria has become a deeply divided nation, with the divisions caused by the religions that were supposed to spread the love. To add to this, rebel groups with conflicting interests needlessly extend the war. I lost hope when I realized that at the end of the day, the fools are holding the guns and the sensible people are running for their lives."

Suddenly, they heard a loud blast at a distance. Salim slowed down the vehicle and secretly parked it near a deserted building. He suggested that they should better wait until the shelling noises had stopped completely.

Adi saw Salim grabbing a water bottle and pouring water all over himself to refresh against the heat and sweat. He felt bad for Salim who was suffering for Adi's cause. He said, "I am really sorry for making you suffer all of this."

Salim smiled. "This is my Motherland sir. It is my duty to serve my guest. Volunteers like you who risk their lives to save strangers are greater than us... And it will be an honour to serve you in any way. Most importantly, doing things like this make me feel passionate and alive… Or I feel useless and wasted in my own soil."

Adi smiled at Salim, and couldn't help but give him a hug. They waited for a while until they were sure that the sounds of shelling were over. And they continued their journey towards Madaya.

"How is this place – this Madaya? Have you been there before?" Adi asked.

"Madaya used to be a weekend retreat for people like us, sir. It's a small mountainous city with special weather completely different from the rest of the neighbourhood. But ever since the war has begun, it is besieged by loyal Syrian forces and Lebanese militia, Hezbollah. So, it has become difficult for anyone to get in or out of that place. But don't worry, sir… We shall work out something to find our way through."

Salim's bold attitude heartened Adi. But his concern for Nila, who was probably in a mountain town locked in war, started to disturb him insistently again. He knew that it would be wrong to push Salim to drive faster, but Salim would understand him and would not abandon him if he did that.

Adi wanted to ask how much longer they'd need to travel, when a bomb from nowhere landed directly in front of their ambulance, throwing them into the air along with the ambulance. Adi and Salim were flung away into the loose sand, making them escape the blast unhurt. They were lying on the ground, feeling the mysterious silence in the unsettled dust all over the place. The ambulance, unfortunately, got struck into a crater caused by the bomb.

***

Adi and Salim were on the ground, thankful to be alive. But they were not in a position to get the ambulance back onto the road. So they decided to take a pause before proceeding with their next course of action. The shelling continued across the area, making their lives more dangerous by the minute. Salim pointed to a deserted building, which used to be a famous school and suggested taking shelter there.

They walked into the building clandestinely, and took shelter, trying not to make much noise. The remnants of drawings and instructions on the blackboard were a testament to the sorry state of affairs in the country. They saw shelling remnants and bullet marks all across the classrooms. Adi feared the worst, but Salim knew it was.

"It doesn't end with the bombings, bullets, and airstrikes. Now they have started this chemical warfare, which makes one starve for oxygen, resulting in the most horrible death which mankind had ever witnessed," said Salim.

"Why is no other country doing anything about it?" asked Adi, agitated by Salim's words and the ruined classrooms.

"Well, I don't know, sir. They seem to be busy with their own problems of supremacy. Super-power nations simply refuse to acknowledge a world beyond them. They could have ignored us and stopped funding the war... If they had not acted for their own gains and incensed the warring factions, this war would have died naturally. But they didn't do it."

As they were walking through the place, Adi noticed some writing on one of the boards.

'When you tell a lie, you steal someone's right to truth. But what if you tell it to yourself?'

Below the wordings, a name was scrawled in bold.

'The Mind Society'

"What is that?" asked Adi.

"I don't know... I have heard the name somewhere, but I'm not sure what exactly it is."

Adi and Salim came to the centre of the school, where they noticed that the place had been used very recently. Remains of food and water packets were scattered on the floor.

Although Adi was hesitant to walk further, Salim insisted that they should move ahead, as they had no other choice but to look for help, even if it came from an enemy.

Salim opened the door of one of the deserted classroom in the ground floor. It was spotless for a place attacked in the war. They both fell silent, hearing some noises coming from somewhere nearby. Adi's heart was pounding, but Salim remained composed, as he knew that hideouts were for civilians and not for militants.

He saw a little elevation on the floor and realized that it was actually a sliding door to the underground. Salim opened the door silently, despite Adi warning him not to. He slowly descended into the area, but Adi was still standing above ground, unable to proceed. After a while, Salim came back near the doors and showed double thumbs up signal, and got back underground.

Adi placing all his trust on a pair of thumbs, climbed down the stairs to witness a strange sight. The underground room was filled with people seated on the floor, with their eyes closed. A bearded man was leading them into a trance, attempting hypnosis through his commentary.

***

Adi and Salim looked at the bearded man, standing amidst the group of people who were seated on the floor in a meditative state. The man signalled them to go back and wait without disturbing the proceedings.

Adi sat on the disfigured sofa placed at the back of the room. Salim just stood there, keenly listening to the commentary. Adi initially thought it was a religious discourse for the people in pain.

But as he started listening closely, the words sounded totally weird to him.

They sounded like a description of an exquisite place, and a fantasy life filled with abundance. The bearded man continued to speak about the land of overwhelming peace and happiness, and the people listening to him started smiling in their trance.

It was just the first day for Adi in Syria, but he had seen things that would last a lifetime. He promised himself to tackle all the pain of the journey, and never cease until he had found Nila.

He knew that he had been living more on impulses, one act at a time, rather than a complete conscience, which he had lost after losing Nila and his memory.

The commentary continued for another fifteen minutes, after which the bearded man requested the people to sit in groups of three, and discuss their experiences and share their happiness.

Adi was perplexed, wondering if this was some kind of an asylum. The people were impossibly happy, considering the country they were living in. He saw the bearded man approaching them with a smile. This made Adi quite anxious about what to speak, but thankfully, Salim was ready with his questions.

"Were you referred by Aref Dalila?" the man asked, looking at Salim.

"No, sir. We are volunteers at the hospital, but we lost our way due to a bomb strike…" Salim said and introduced himself and Adi.

"Very well then, you are in a safe place as of now. I am Dr. Ali. I was working as a professor at Damascus University until a few years ago but now I am a volunteer like you. I am slightly selfish, as I have restricted my services to my own people at present."

"That's not selfish, Professor. It's a priority," replied Salim.

Dr. Ali smiled. "You made my day, Salim."

Turning to Adi, he said, "I have been to your country, and I challenge that there can never be another country like India with so much diversity, and yet stand united. Look at us… Ours is a small nation with limited differences, and yet we are stubborn on burning it down to ashes."

Dr. Ali sat on the sofa and grabbed a water bottle. He gestured to the people smiling in the room. "For an old professor like me… I think this is all I can do. Bring happiness to their hearts."

"What exactly is happening here, Professor?" Adi asked, breaking his silence.

The professor looked at Adi and smiled. "Don't you have something called Virtual Reality or Artificial Intelligence in your country?"

Adi nodded, unable to place the context here.

"Well, this is our cheaper version of it. Copyrights are pending though," Dr. Ali laughed at his own joke.

Salim couldn't follow the conversation but smiled along, not giving away that he could not get the context.

Dr. Ali, however, knew that he had a big explanation to give. He sipped some more water, sat back on the sofa, and started. "My people are suffering in silence. I see it as an illness that needs to be cured... Or I fear even this pain will become an addiction. Drugs and alcohol aren't the only things that people can get addicted to. Even abuse and suffering can become an addiction at a deeper psychological level. Oscillating between extremes is addictive, and people start relying on the drug – like high that follows, whenever the abuse stops..."

Salim listened carefully, feeling that the professor was complicating a simple feeling. "Even assuming the addiction part to be true, what's wrong with that? Do they have any choice in this country?"

"It's not that simple, Salim. Addicts get their feelings numbed over time and this is too dangerous a trait. I don't want that to happen to my people. I am fighting this addiction, and I am sure it is helping people."

"What exactly do you do, Professor? And what are these people doing?" Salim asked, refusing to believe that there could be a solution to people's fear and agony.

"Listen, Salim, I am trying to help only those people who want to be helped. You could say it's a war zone treatment, for people with mental suffering. I don't have much time for any research before getting this started. You see the people smiling here... Don't you think this means success to me? If not this, you'd see them killing themselves... Or worse, killing others out of sheer mental imbalance," Dr. Ali said firmly.

Salim became quiet, as didn't want to sound sceptical anymore. He had himself seen cases of suicides and murder amidst the war injuries and death.

Dr. Ali decided to explain about The Mind Society to Salim and Adi, thinking that might help them, or someone else in need through them.

"Everything we experience in this world goes through one filter – that's our mind. Our mind and memories keep evolving with time. The Mind Society tries to divert the minds of these people from war, and let them create something beautiful to dwell upon. At the end of the day, no matter whoever you are, death is natural, but fear is not. This relative feeling of fear in itself is an indication that people's feelings oscillate easily. And this is something I decided to tap on."

"So you are saying these people are trying to create a false world and convince themselves that it's real…" Salim asked, who was surprised by the logic of The Mind Society.

Dr. Ali smiled. "As I said, it's all up to you. You are your world. The real difference, I must say, lies in a person's capacity to live in an imaginary world. I remember my earlier life when I would keenly look forward to Friday evenings.

"But then I realized, even a Monday evening is just the same, except that our minds process more than just the present to come up with a complicated but stubborn belief. It's up to you to change the belief and make yourself happy all the time."

"I got your logic, sir. But tell me how effective is this?" Salim asked.

"As they say, 100 percent commitment is easier than 98 percent commitment"

Adi kept listening to Dr. Ali who continued.

"Look at you… You have come here to volunteer, leaving behind a reasonably comfortable life, I presume. However, right this moment, you are living the exact same life as these people.

"The only thing that makes you feel better or superior is the belief that you will go back and lead a comfortable life again. But according to me, that is an illusion until it actually happens. Why shouldn't I bring the same superior belief into my people, by the same illusion?"

"Thank you, Professor!" Salim said, moved by Dr. Ali's efforts. "I just can't imagine anything better than this for Syria now, and I am happy it is happening. But don't you think when people are in sizeable groups, this belief might be questioned at some point?"

"Good question. Madness is rare in individuals… But in groups and crowds, it is the rule. So I am using that to my benefit. I am teaching madness here, but for a good cause though…"

Salim smiled, "After all this explanation I don't think I would fit the bill in joining the madness, would I?"

"Why not? Do you think I am keeping these people confounded under darkness? I discuss everything with them, like how I discussed with you. But the success of this depends on the practice and trust they show. It's like the trust one has on God."

Adi was amazed at the clarity Dr. Ali had in making a complex thought sound so simple. He wondered how wonderful people like him still existed amidst all the chaos, and continued doing amazing service without losing any sheen. The more he talked with Dr. Ali, the bigger his love and respect for the professor became. He poured out all his problems, worries and anxiety to Dr. Ali and felt uniquely peaceful, just like how he had felt with Raj Purniman.

Dr. Ali invited Adi and Salim for dinner that night with his group and suggested that they shall discuss the next course of action to find Nila. The food, which was prepared with a limited supply of ingredients, was relatively simple but was made more memorable by the stories people shared during the dinner.

One of the members told the gathering that, more than anything, the group in itself showed him happiness, as everyone was keen on helping everyone else.

Another person told the group that he used to be the cameraman for a local television channel before the war, and after joining The Mind Society he felt like he was operating his mind just like he used to operate his camera.

He suggested the group to be more dynamic in their imaginations, as he felt that more details added more authenticity to the imagination. He also emphasized his belief that beauty is not in the static simplicity of the art but in the dynamic imagination it provokes.

The talks were a revelation for Salim, who had never seen such optimism and happiness in his country ever since the war had started.

Dr. Ali told the group to become children once more and fill their mind with fairy tales the way the kids would do, and start believing in them. He believed everyone was a kid by heart. It was just that their beliefs and joys became complex and bigger with time.

Adi introduced himself to the group and discussed how much he felt at peace at that place, even amidst all the sorrows surrounding it.

He discussed his reason for visiting Syria, and his plans to visit Madaya. One of the people from the group informed Adi that his friend was in charge of the security at Madaya and that he could help Adi get inside the mountain city. Dr.

Ali decided to accompany Adi to Madaya, as he felt that he could be of some help to Adi and to the people suffering in Madaya.

***

✦✦✦

She Lived Between the Lines

A small vehicle, disguised as army truck, started its journey in the early hours from the vandalized school near Aleppo, towards the besieged town of Madaya. Dr. Ali and Adi were seated at the back, with Salim driving.

"Thank you for accompanying me. I'm grateful. But I feel it is way too risky for an important man like you to undertake this journey," Adi said.

"Not at all. This is how I want to live until I die. I want my life to preach more than my lips. Most importantly, this is still my country, and I would convince myself taking a weekend break to Madaya for partying." said Dr. Ali, laughing heartily above the vehicle's noisy drone.

"I feel so many emotions right now, but guilt dominates them all. It's like I am on a rough roller coaster ride, anxious about my lost wife," said Adi.

Dr. Ali shook his head, patted Adi's shoulders, and said, "Don't worry, son. Everything will be alright."

The simple endearment brought out all the sadness that Adi had been compressing within. Dr. Ali hugged him. "You are not alone in this, son. We are all with you. Don't doubt humanity just because a handful of maniacs are hiding your view."

Adi composed himself and took a sip of water from the can when Dr. Ali asked him to show Nila's picture if he had one right then. Adi opened his wallet and showed him a picture of Nila. His own picture fell from the open wallet. Dr. Ali bent down to pick up Adi's picture, feeling disturbed as he looked at it.

"When was this picture taken?"

"On the day of my marriage," Adi replied.

"Did you even see your face in the mirror recently? You look feeble… I am sure your ribs will stick out if you remove your shirt," Dr. Ali said, concerned.

Adi remained silent for a while, looking at Nila's picture.

"Sir, as I told you, nothing interests me anymore. I want to see the world with her, and also through her. She would get excited about little things. And that encouraged me to create little things for her every day. If we go to a movie theatre, I would rather watch her face which, for me, is more interesting than any movie. Every day I look forward to doing something which can surprise her and bring her happiness. But today she is lost, and she has taken away my life with her as well. I just cannot accept life until I find her." Adi said, wiping his tears.

Dr. Ali's eyes got moist as well, and he tried to diffuse the sadness. "Okay, whatever it is, first help yourself, and try to eat something. Or else your Nila might think that some malnourished Syrian farmer has come to kidnap her…"

Adi smiled at the joke, feeling forlorn inside.

The journey lasted throughout the day, as they couldn't drive fast on the roads rampaged by the war. The occasional checkpoints were crossed with ease, either by using Adi's volunteer card or by Dr. Ali's homemade defence card. The vehicle finally neared Madaya, and Salim pointed out "Madaya ", the small mountain town to Adi whose excitement spiked up. He tried hard to contain his emotions, but his eyes betrayed him shamelessly.

They reached the checkpoint where their arrival was already intimated to the officials via the person from The Mind Society. Dr. Ali and Adi were allowed to enter Madaya, but Salim was asked to stay back. Salim didn't resist, as he understood their current situation.

"Why do you even come here? Once you enter, there is no guarantee that you would come out in one piece. You can't even escape the landmines planted all around," the soldier who was helping them enter Madaya asked them wonderingly. He had to skip his rest time and do overtime duty just to be present at the check post to allow Adi and Dr. Ali to enter the hills.

Dr. Ali asked for Nila's photo, saying it would help until they found Nila. Adi handed over the picture to him. He requested Adi to wait at the gates, as he wanted to have a little private discussion with the soldier, to get a hang of things in Madaya.

Adi held Dr. Ali's hands. "I am feeling numb, sir. This place terrifies me. I just can't believe my Nila is here. Will she be alright?"

Dr. Ali smiled and held Adi's shoulders. "Be positive. It's the only choice you have. It will broaden your perspective, and let you see things better."

He then left Adi at the gates to talk with the soldier. Adi noticed from a distance that the discussion grew serious with time. At one point he heard Dr. Ali shouting at the soldier. Adi grew restless and rushed towards the check post but Dr. Ali was already walking out from there.

"Is everything alright?" Adi asked, suspecting something serious.

"How can everything be alright in Syria? He told me six children died of malnutrition yesterday, bringing the total to sixty deaths in one month. And yet, no aid is allowed inside

Madaya. It's been four months since these people received any aid, and now they have started eating rodents, insects, and plants. This is not my country anymore..." Dr. Ali shouted.

Adi understood his state of mind and decided not to ask if he had enquired about Nila. It sounded inappropriate in the bigger scheme of things.

Dr. Ali and Adi began to walk uphill slowly as instructed. Dr. Ali was speaking to himself and looked annoyed by the situation in Madaya. But Adi was feeling calmer that he was close to the end of his search, in a place where hunger was a bigger killer than bullets.

Nila was not in gory danger if she was here. She could survive the wilderness better than anyone he knew.

After covering some distance, Dr. Ali couldn't control himself. He turned and shook his fists at the check post, saying, "Why don't you understand that you will die, too? Why are you doing things that you don't like? Stop it before it kills you!"

Adi held him gently, helping him along the way

***

Adi couldn't speak a word. He was overwhelmed by the atmosphere and the emotions. Dr. Ali tried to divert Adi's mind by speaking about philosophies, but Adi's mind was focused elsewhere.

The town was empty for the first few hundred meters, after which they could see some dense concrete structures, indicating that it had been a busy area once. Most of the structures were damaged by war, and there was an unearthly silence.

As they both walked further inside, they saw a few children, who had been hiding behind a building, running towards them.

Dr. Ali asked Adi to wait as he wanted to speak to the little ones. The kids came closer, they raised their hands, begging for food. They looked worn out, and like they were used to begging for food.

Dr. Ali hugged a couple of the kids and said, "I am sorry, children. I don't have anything with me now, but I promise to get you lots of food the next time."

He was unable to see the disappointment in the children's face and felt deep grief seeing the condition of the children. He was angry and sad, but more than that, the helplessness hurt him worse. He sat down near a building and remained silent for a while before continuing to walk.

Dr. Ali noticed two old men staring at them from a distance. He started speaking to them from afar so they didn't feel threatened. Once nearer, he said that they had come there to help the people of Madaya and that they were taking an estimate of the damage and noting down the needs of the people for getting the aid.

The old men got excited and opened up all about the war and the struggles they faced. Dr. Ali listened to them for a while, and before they could come up with further stories, he gently thanked them, indicating that he had got all the necessary information.

He also said that he would need to make some more rounds of the town before getting back to the Capital. While leaving, Dr. Ali enquired about Heba's house and got the details.

"Who is Heba?" asked Adi.

"Heba is the name of a little girl who lost her eyesight due to the war. Her story became a sensation in the world media. I wanted to meet her family," Dr. Ali said sadly.

"Sir, what about Nila? I thought we came here to find her!"

"Listen, Adi... We must get to know the people here first, and earn their trust so they would lead us to Nila." Dr. Ali explained.

Adi was confused. He felt that this move was completely unnecessary. "But why is that even needed? Can't they tell you what they know? We're suffering too. They could help us, one human to another."

Dr. Ali stopped walking and turned to Adi, who looked pale.

"You have reached this far, Adi. This is a miracle in itself. Why don't you wait some more? Please don't ask me any more questions... You know I am here just for you."

Adi nodded but he was nervous and sweating profusely. Even his walk was clumsy.

Dr. Ali was following the path as guided by the old men and found himself at a junction where he was uncertain of the further route. He saw that two of the kids who had begged him for food were following them. He called them closer. "Do you know Heba's house?"

"Heba, the blind one?" asked one of the boys.

Dr. Ali nodded. They were further guided by the boys to a house which looked interestingly unique amidst the broken concrete structures. It was like a little oasis in the troubled war zone, owing to the plants that were growing all around the house.

The kids pointed to a pomegranate tree near the house, which was perhaps the only tree that had lived through the war in the town. The kids ran back into town after telling them that Heba played here all the time.

Dr. Ali slowly walked near the doors, looking all around the place and gently knocking on it. The door was open and the house looked way too small from the inside but spotless and beautiful. As Dr. Ali explored the house, Adi found it too disturbing inside and was unable to stay in. He rushed out and walked towards the pomegranate tree, trying to calm himself. Dr. Ali was surprised to see Adi's reaction. He followed Adi and stood beside him.

"Why are you restless? I told you to be positive…"

Adi mutely shook his head, trying to compose himself. Dr. Ali patted Adi gently and walked back to the house. Adi was in a state of sleepless despair. He lay down below the pomegranate tree and fell asleep instantly. He slept for hours together. When he opened his eyes, it was already dark. He noticed that Dr. Ali was talking to an old couple, and they were all seated outside the house.

Seeing Adi approaching them, the old couple stood up with their hands folded. Dr. Ali urged them to sit down again. Adi didn't speak a word but acknowledged the old couple's greetings.

"This is Mr. Rashid and his wife. Heba is their granddaughter." Dr. Ali introduced them.

Adi nodded but he was in no mood to talk. Dr. Ali was worried. Adi looked too unpredictable and depressed. He decided to divert Adi's mind, not bothering about how he reacted.

"Heba's parents were one among the first to escape Syria. They tried to climb the mountain to enter Lebanon, but unfortunately, they couldn't fight the snow and were frozen to death. It was a miracle that someone found Heba alive, given her condition.

"The way she fought back the frost bites to live to this day is a fantastic example of her grit and determination. She was handed over to her grandparents, who were reluctant to leave this place initially. But now they are stuck here even though they wish to move out." Dr. Ali detailed.

Adi turned and saw Heba sleeping inside the house.

"Is she alright?" He asked, concerned.

"She is better now. She was sick before," Rashid replied in his feeble voice.

"What happened?"

This time Dr. Ali intruded, not wanting Rashid to strain. "It's some kind of viral infection which eventually made her weak, by the loss of appetite and dehydration."

Rashid added, "There is only one medical centre here, but it has plenty of patients. Only a few volunteers are helping them round the clock, and unfortunately, even the critical ones are not allowed to be taken to the main hospitals."

Adi could see the sorrow in the eyes of the old couple. They had nobody other than a little blind granddaughter. Rashid and his wife were yet to come to terms with the war.

They were not agile enough to understand things and didn't know anything but their regular life, which they insisted on continuing despite the hostile environment.

As Rashid was partially deaf, Dr. Ali raised his voice to ask, "How do you manage things?"

Rashid smiled and pointed to the sky, indicating that Allah would take care of it all.

"I can't work anymore. There is no more work to do either. I can't run to get food from the aid truck, but somebody or the other gets us something to eat and keeps us alive. You see... It's not just me. Everybody has a sad story here, so we understand each other without a word."

As the talk continued, three youngsters appeared before them from the darkness.

***

"Don't panic sir, it's me, Salim. These are my friends..." One of the men called out.

Salim had entered Madaya surreptitiously with the help of his friends.

"But why would you do that?" asked Dr. Ali, taken aback by their sudden entry.

"I was in the vehicle outside, when I noticed these guys trying to enter the town. It was only after a little discussion with them that I realized the sad state of affairs here. I thought about you people and decided to be of some help here, so I joined them."

"I think except for the food and medical supplies, things are getting better here," said Dr. Ali, trying to convince the youngsters.

"That's too easily said, sir said Issam, one of the guys who had accompanied Salim. "What about dealing with the weather here? We don't have fuel to warm ourselves. The protracted cold weather and darkness without power are causing uncontrolled misery despite bringing us together."

Dr. Ali felt sorry for not thinking of this.

"But where did you go?" he asked, looking at Issam this time.

"Every day is terrifying here. So we decided to stop calculating the risk and escaped the town in search of food. We grabbed some supplies from the nearby town, and came back to give it to our people."

"Do you think that is enough for your people?" asked Adi, seeing the size of the packet in Issam's hand.

"This is enough for my little nephew. I hope this would get him back into action at least for a couple of days," replied Issam, trying to control himself.

"I am sorry," said Adi, holding Issam's hand. His eyes were moist as well. He stood up and walked towards the house to see Heba. She was smiling in her sleep.

"Does she have anything to eat?" Adi asked.

"Yes, we have enough for her. We cannot let her starve, she is all we have now," Rashid replied.

Issam opened his packet and handed one bread packet to Rashid. "You should eat something too."

Rashid's wife, however, declined the offer and told everyone to wait so she could make some soup for them.

"Gone are days when we used to run around every day for a living. Today we are hiding to live. Justice is just dead," Issam exclaimed in frustration.

"Justice is just another invention of man, Issam. It's rarely achievable, oftentimes impractical and subjective. But still, many people will not hesitate to destroy lives demanding it. This is exactly what is happening here," said Dr. Ali.

"Then we must avenge those who have died."

"Can it bring back peace? It will just be a brutal desecration of their memory," Dr. Ali countered.

"So you mean no revenge must be sought? What else do you think we should do?" Issam asked angrily.

"Listen, I understand your feelings. But our anger just reveals the weakness of character and thirst for violence. Revenge is for petty and irresponsible people. Youngsters like you have a nation to rebuild from scratch. So better start saving all that can be saved, starting with the lives of the people who are still alive and trying to live."

The animated discussion continued for a while until they had soup made from homegrown tomatoes. Adi was in no mood to eat, but he took a little for the sake of the old couple, and excused himself from the gathering, telling them that he wanted some rest.

Rashid's wife said to him, "You need to sleep. Try sleeping with a good thought, you will wake up with the same thought."

Adi gave a tired smile and requested for a bed that he could put under the pomegranate tree. Adi refused to get inside the house, despite everyone's requests and slept under the tree.

But he could not close his eyes due to the turmoil in his mind. His eyes remained wet as he lay awake, listening to the discussion outside throughout the night.

***

Finally, Adi drifted off to sleep, unaware of the additional blankets that were spread over him during the night. It was early in the morning when Adi felt someone touching his feet. He pushed aside the blanket to see Heba standing in front of him.

Knowing that Adi was awake, she smiled and said, "I am Heba, I came to visit you."

"Hey Heba, It's too early in the morning. You must go back to sleep now. By the way, how are you feeling?" Adi asked her. He touched her forehead which was still warm.

"You are still sick. You must take rest. Let me get you back inside," Adi said, getting up from his bed.

"Not now, please. I came to speak to you. I was afraid that you will leave without seeing me," Heba said.

Adi was unable to comprehend the depth of the little girl's love.

"How can I leave without meeting you? I came here just to see you."

"Is this pomegranate tree happy?" Heba asked, touching its bark.

"I think it is happy now. It was sad before, as you didn't speak to it yesterday," Adi replied with a smile that did not touch his eyes.

Adi saw Heba's smile as she hugged and kissed the pomegranate tree.

"Do you know me, Heba?" Adi's voice broke.

Heba didn't answer him directly, but smiled, saying, "I like you."

Adi held Heba's little hands. "What else do you like?"

"Well, I like this pomegranate tree, my little plants, their flowers, my clay dolls, and the beautiful view from here," she said.

"Oh really, what view is that?" Adi asked, swallowing his tears.

"There are big and beautiful mountains out there, and a small lake at the bottom called Barada, where little kids like me are playing all the time. There is a snowy peak where kids like me go once we grow up, and can get our wish fulfilled." Heba explained in her excited voice.

"So, you have your wishes ready?"

"Yes, I had a wish ready before, but now I have a different wish..."

"And what wish is that?" Adi asked, wiping his tears.

"I am not supposed to say that. But tell me... How long will it take for me to grow big?" she asked, holding Adi's hand this time.

Adi composed himself and said, "It will take a while, but right now I can go and make that wish for you."

His tears fell on Heba's hand. She became quiet, walked into the house and came back with something in her hand.

"I have brought a gift for you," she said, handing over a little toy girl to him.

Adi looked at it, feeling a strange stirring in his stomach. "You made this?"

"No, but I take care of her and get her to sleep every night."

"What's her name?"

Heba did not reply. She just kissed the doll and cried.

"I don't need this toy, Heba. I have plenty like this at home. But you must promise me something before I give it back." Adi said.

Heba wordlessly hugged Adi with her little arms.

"You must take care of yourself, Heba. You must get stronger and continue to love everything and everyone around you, like you do now."

Heba refused to let go of Adi and continued to cry on his shoulders.

Adi held Heba tight and was crying on her little shoulders and said with a broken voice. "I know your wish for the mountains, Heba. I also know the name of the toy"

Heba cried, "Please get her back. I want her."

Adi sobbed and screamed at the sky. "NILA! I am sorry, Nila. I was late. Please forgive me."

Dr. Ali, Salim, and the old couple who had been crying behind the doors of the house rushed out. They hugged Adi, not letting the sorrow engulf him. They cried with him hugging each other. It was a different country with different people and yet Adi felt like he belonged there, and they had known him forever.

Adi hugged Heba to his chest, realising that he was not the only one who missed Nila. He kissed Heba's little hands, and asked her, "Will you come home with me? I need a strong person like you to be with me…"

Heba sobbed softly. "But I have that wish to make!"

"You want Nila back, isn't that your wish?" asked Adi, wiping Heba's tears gently with his thumbs.

Heba nodded.

"She is inside you and me, Heba, and also inside these little toys of ours…"

Heba smiled wanly, "I will come with you…"

She handed him a piece of folded paper that she had been clutching safely in her hands, something she was supposed to have given him before.

Dr. Ali held Adi's hands. "I am sorry for your loss, son. I am ashamed that it happened in my soil…"

But Adi was consumed by a grief so profound that nothing penetrated the wall of desolate sadness that seemed to envelop him. But he knew he had to console the older man.

"Please don't, sir! You are a good human. You need not be sorry. All the people I have seen so far in this soil are angels. You must be proud of your homeland. A little girl showed so much strength in disclosing the truth… Believe me, I am nothing in front of her. I felt betrayed and angry at everything until yesterday night. But now everything makes sense. I realized that ever since I woke up from the accident, everyone and everything was preparing me for this loss. The more I think about it, the more it makes sense. I am thankful to all of you, and life itself."

***

The others moved aside to give him privacy. With his heart thumping, Adi opened the letter.

Dear Adi,

I just can't believe I am writing this, Adi. I wanted to come out to find you but got stuck here. The war has become severe. Trying to escape this place means sure death. That is why I decided to write this letter. If you are reading this, I presume there is good news, and bad news.

The good news is that you are alive, and you came back for me. What took you so long, Adi? I missed you all the time.

The bad news is that I am no more. As I write this, a strange feeling engulfs me when I think I am no more. For a village girl like me, I feel I have come a long way, Adi. I was that frog in the well, swimming in circles until you took me out to the sea.

I can't express how much I have gone through, ever since you left me here. I have carried dead children to wailing parents, away from where they were killed...

Worse still, I saw some dying in front of me. I get only nightmares now. After seeing so much bloodshed and death, I had almost grown immune to this.

I also feel that my time is nearing. But the thought of you coming back for me keeps me alive. I hope I could see you at least one more time, Adi. But if you are reading this, then I didn't make it.

With every passing day, I am becoming one among these people. They love me and care for me. The longer I stayed with them the better I realized that they are just like us.

It's not the death these people fear, but the uncertainty about their future. They feel they have something more important left to do before they die. But living amidst them, I felt I am doing it already.

In the middle of all this drama, there are some special people who live in their own beautiful world. They are the little children I am taking care of here. They make me forget everything… And whenever I see them, I wonder how fragile they are.

But it's that fragility that makes them live life fully unmindful of sadness or joy. I can only try to eliminate the kids' boredom here, Adi. I couldn't do much about their hunger, or the suffering they undergo every day.

There is one more person in my life now, and it's because of her that I feel peace at the end of the day. She is Heba, a little blind girl who cannot see the crimes of war. But she created her own beautiful world and invites me into it, too.

We both love gardening and making clay toys together. We share our stories and dreams. I have told her a lot about you, and she is too eager to meet you. I hope she would be the one who gives you this letter.

She is too precious, Adi. Please protect her and her dreams if she is still alive when you read this.

I must say I am the luckiest girl in the world, Adi. I remember how stupid I had been all this while… And yet, I don't remember a single instance when you wanted me to be different.

You became my forest, and my rain, accepting me the way I am.

Everybody loves me, and you brought me to everybody, out of that little world I was keeping myself in.

Thanks for being there for me. From a forest girl who never looked beyond the mountains, to a girl who has seen everything, you have made my life memorable.

I have started seeing every single day as a new chance, a little life by itself. Every morning is a little birth, and every night a little death. This way, I feel I am living more and preparing myself for the inevitable.

I understood nothing is fair in love and war, but I am afraid of not seeing you anymore.

Whenever I am in a panic, I remember your words, in my early days in the city, saying that you will be somewhere in the crowd with your eyes always on me.

These words keep me going, Adi. I don't even want this letter to come to an end... I feel I am speaking with you while writing this.

I miss you, Adi. I miss you a lot. I miss your messy hair and your hiccoughing laughter.

I keep cursing myself for sending you to get aid for people here, or you would have been with me. I want to talk a lot with you. I had planned so many surprises for your birthday but I am afraid that might not happen.

Okay, if you are reading this, it didn't happen. I do not know where you went, or what happened to you. But every day, I wake up expecting you to be next to me. That has not happened until today.

Adi, I feel that my life has been a fairy tale, with mountains, love, journeys and now, war. Even my death will become a story. All of this is like a prolonged dream, Adi. But when two people who are together have the same dream, it becomes our reality. Thanks for dreaming with me.

Thanks for loving a reckless soul like me so deeply that even I have fallen in love with myself. That feeling is enough forever. And yes, whenever you miss me, remember I will be watching you from afar.

But sorry, there will be tears.

I love you, Adi. Please take care.

Nila

Adi sat there with the letter, his tears dripping all over it. He saw Heba approaching him with a flower in her hand. He closed his eyes, took a deep breath, and smiled at her. He got the flower and placed it at a small tombstone beside the pomegranate tree.

The inscription read,

'For the girl who came from somewhere and taught us how to live – Nila.'

✦ ✦ ✦

About the Author

Santhosh Sivaraj prefers seeing with the mind, writing with the heart, and living through others. This way, he believes, he gets to live more of life, per life. He has worn many hats in life; that of a Sailor, a Banker, an Entrepreneur, and even a Teacher. But his belief in considering life's journey to be a destination in itself pushes him to seek further avenues in life. Absurd economics interests him and he loves doing stand-up comedy to his loved ones. He laughs at his own mistakes and loves life unconditionally.